"I'm not really your wife."

"That can soon be fixed." Ethan's eyes flickered to her shocked face. "I think we'd both like that." He reached out and touched Hannah's cheek, his fingers leaving a trail of fire against her skin.

"You look as if I've made an improper suggestion." Ethan continued. "We're married, nothing could be more proper than for us to share a bed."

Rubbing her cheek against his hand, she closed her eyes. "This wasn't part of the deal."

"Circumstances change, situations alter. If you're going to fall in love, it might as well be with me."

KIM LAWRENCE lives on a farm in rural Anglesey, Wales. She runs two miles daily and finds this an excellent opportunity to unwind and seek inspiration for her writing! It also helps her keep up with her husband, two active sons and the various stray animals which have adopted them. Always a fanatical consumer of fiction, she is now equally enthusiastic about writing. She loves a happy ending!

Kim Lawrence

WIFE BY AGREEMENT

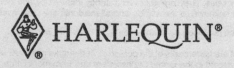

TORONTO • NEW YORK • LONDON
AMSTERDAM • PARIS • SYDNEY • HAMBURG
STOCKHOLM • ATHENS • TOKYO • MILAN • MADRID
PRAGUE • WARSAW • BUDAPEST • AUCKLAND

ISBN 0-373-12147-4

WIFE BY AGREEMENT

First North American Publication 2000.

This edition published by arrangement with Harlequin Books S.A.

® and TM are trademarks of the publisher. Trademarks indicated with
® are registered in the United States Patent and Trademark Office, the
Canadian Trade Marks Office and in other countries.

Visit us at www.eHarlequin.com

Printed in U.S.A.

CHAPTER ONE

HANNAH slid the key very carefully into the lock. Inside the only sound was the ticking of the clock. Nobody was up, thank goodness. She leant back against the door and gave a slow sigh of relief—at last!

She didn't bother switching on the light, but slipped thankfully out of the remains of her patent leather court shoes. Tucking them under her arm, she felt her way carefully past the big scrubbed table that had centre stage in the room. She thought with longing of a hot, cleansing shower. The sudden illumination made her freeze and blink like a startled animal.

'Is all this subterfuge really necessary? There isn't a curfew.' Ethan had moved to sit at the table, a half-empty glass of brandy in front of him. The vaguely bored irony faded dramatically from his voice as he took in her bedraggled state. 'What the hell has happened?'

The last thing Hannah felt like was reliving the past hour, and the last person she wanted to explain to was Ethan. Her hand went self-consciously to the torn material of her shirt lapel, but her attempts to hold the fabric together only drew his attention to the pale skin the rent exposed. What was he doing sitting in the dark anyway? She grimaced as she risked a swift glance down.

The unkind electric lights revealed it was even worse than she had thought. Her legs were covered with mud and her fine denier tights were in shreds; her velvet skirt was torn in several places and the pale skin of her shoulders and midriff showed through the gaping tears in her silk shirt.

'It looks a lot worse than it is,' she said soothingly. It didn't feel it, though. The scratches on her cheek were beginning to sting as the warmth of the room thawed her cold body. There was a promise of winter in the autumn air tonight.

With an impatient gesture Ethan dismissed her weak attempt to pacify him. 'Have you been in a car crash?'

'Not exactly.' You couldn't call jumping out of a car moving at thirty miles an hour a crash, exactly. She had a pretty good idea what Ethan would call it—insanity, probably. He hadn't been there, though. It had been— A deep shudder rippled through her body and she swayed as the whole room pitched.

Ethan reached out and touched her arm. 'My God, you're like ice.' He took off his robe and wrapped it around her. 'Sit down before you fall down.' He pressed her into a chair.

The nausea passed and Hannah opened her eyes. 'You'll get cold,' she protested. Under the robe Ethan was wearing a pair of dark blue pyjama trousers and nothing else. They'd taken the children to the South of France in June, and she noticed irrelevantly that his olive-toned skin was still tanned a deep golden brown.

'Drink this.' She tried to turn her head away as her nostrils flared against the scent of raw alcohol. 'Do as I say.'

It was only under duress that she obeyed; brandy wasn't a taste she'd ever acquired.

'Now tell me exactly what happened.'

'I want a shower,' she fretted. A hand on her shoulders prevented her from rising.

'After I've had my explanation. I was under the impression that you were going out for a meal with your fellow night-class members.' His sceptical tone made it sound as though this was an elaborate lie.

Why would she need to lie to him? Did he think she led a double life or something? 'I was…I did.' She raised her eyes to his face and read implacability there. Best just get it over with. 'Debbie and Alan took me.' Ethan had met the young couple who were learning French with her and he nodded briefly. 'Craig Finch, he only joined the class last month, offered to bring me home. He said it wasn't out of his way and it would save Alan a detour.' She swallowed hard. 'Only Craig took a detour, and when I mentioned it he…he…'

'What did he do?' He spoke quietly, but Ethan Kemp's grey eyes had narrowed to slits and a nerve throbbed erratically in his lean cheek.

'He laughed.' She felt sick just thinking about the expression in Craig's eyes. She'd already been tense—some of the things he'd been saying had been particularly personal, and slimily coarse—but it had been that smile that had really set the alarm bells ringing.

'Laughed?' Ethan echoed incredulously. It wasn't what he'd expected to hear.

'You weren't there!' she shot back angrily. 'He'd been…saying *things*.' In a large group, Craig's behaviour had been unexceptionable, but once he'd got Hannah alone his entire attitude had changed. Everything he'd said had been laced with grubby innuendo. Her frigid silence hadn't put him off at all.

'He hurt you?' Looming over her, Ethan looked a lot more threatening than Craig had been. She felt guilty for making the comparison: Ethan had his faults, but he was a decent man, and no bully, despite the way he was interrogating her right now. Normally he didn't interfere with her life at all.

'No, this happened when I jumped out of the car.'

Some of the repressed violence that had been implicit in his tense stance faded as he stared at her, to be replaced by astonishment. Ethan Kemp wasn't a man easily astonished. His big hands unfurled from the fists they had instinctively formed.

'I don't suppose it was stationary at the time?'

She shook her head and gave him an exasperated look. Ethan wasn't usually so slow. 'I was lucky he hadn't thought to lock the door,' she reflected soberly.

'I can see why you might be thanking your lucky stars,' he agreed drily.

'I landed in brambles and my clothes got a bit ripped getting out,' she explained in a matter-of-fact way. 'I hid in a ditch for a while, just in case he'd followed me, then I walked home over the fields.'

'Where did all this happen?'

'The junction near the Tinkersdale Road.'

'That has to be six miles away.'

'It felt like more, but you're probably right. Her smile was limp at best. 'Don't worry, nobody saw me. Her wide, smooth brow creased as she sought to reassure him. Ethan Kemp's wife strolling through the market town where they lived in this state wouldn't create the sort of image he would approve of, and Ethan cared about the image they presented to the world. Didn't it occur to you to ring me—or the police for that matter?'

'I didn't think to grab my bag; I had no money— nothing. The police aren't interested in crimes that didn't happen. He didn't actually touch me.'

'You're sure he was going to?'

This was an insinuation too far! Anger enabled her to nudge aside the incipient exhaustion that made her eyelids heavy.

'It was one of those occasions when prevention seemed better than cure,' she snapped crisply. The snap seemed to surprise him. Tough, she thought with uncharacteristic venom. Under the circumstances she thought she was being quite restrained. What did he expect her to do? Sit back and wait to be a crime statistic? 'I don't let my imagination run away with me, Ethan.'

This was unarguable: Hannah Smith was the most placid, practical female that he had, in his thirty-six years, ever met. He frowned—after a year's marriage he still thought of her as Hannah Smith, not Kemp. If anyone had suggested to him this morning that she was capable of throwing herself from a moving vehicle he'd have laughed at the absurdity of such an idea.

Hannah was not exactly timid, although her reserved manner made people initially assume she was, but she was not the sort of woman calmly to wade through muddy fields and brambles after extricating herself from a dangerous situation. At least he hadn't thought she was. Would she have told him about it at all if he hadn't witnessed her return? Had she intended appearing at breakfast just as if nothing had happened?

'We should contact the police.'

'Why? Nothing happened. I expect they'd write me off as a neurotic female.' If Ethan could think it, why not total strangers? 'I would like to get my bag back, though—my wallet's in it.'

'Wouldn't you like to see that swine get his just deserts?' he growled incredulously. He found it hard to identify with a turn-the-other-cheek philosophy.

'Like?' she said quietly. She raised her head and at first he didn't realise the tears glistening in her hazel eyes were tears of rage. This only became obvious when she spoke and her voice shook with suppressed fury. 'What I'd *like* to do is make him endure, just for five minutes, the sort of helplessness and terror I...' She bit down hard on her lower lip to stop it trembling. 'We rarely get what we *like*, Ethan.'

'That's a depressing philosophy.' The depth of her

passion shocked him; that she had any passion at all shocked him! More than shocked him—it made him uneasy. What other surprises lurked beneath the placid exterior?

'It's just an observation. Now, if you don't mind I'd like to go to bed.'

He kept a hold on her elbow, as though he expected her to collapse at any moment. At the door of her bedroom she slipped the robe off her shoulders.

'Thank you. Sorry if I got it grubby. Goodnight, Ethan.' This polite, but firm, dismissal appeared to make him change his mind about what he was going to say. She smiled vaguely at him as she disappeared into her bedroom. A few seconds later she heard the sound of Ethan's bedroom door slamming.

Her lip curled with distaste as she stripped. Even if she could have salvaged the clothes, she'd have put them out with the rubbish. As it was they hung off her like rags.

A glance in the full-length cheval-mirror shocked her. Her glossy brown hair had pulled loose of its neat French braid and was liberally anointed with mud. The long scratches along the right side of her face showed through the dirt. The streaks of mascara that gave her the look of a startled panda blended in with the general grime. The amount of flesh exposed through the gaping holes in her shirt was nothing short of indecent. No wonder Ethan had been shocked—she looked appalling!

It was a relief to stand under the hot spray of the shower and let the steamy water wash away some of her tension along with the dirt. It didn't matter how hard she scrubbed, thinking about Craig made her feel grubby. How could a man who seemed so—well, *normal* act like that? Had she given the impression she would welcome such advances? She dismissed this horrifying notion swiftly. No, this hadn't been her fault.

In her *naïveté* she had imagined that a ring on her finger gave a girl automatic protection from unwanted advances. She automatically glanced down at her finger—it looked oddly bare without the slim gold band. On her knees, she searched the floor of the shower cubicle. It wasn't there. Panic out of proportion with the loss flooded through her.

She stepped out of the shower and hastily wrapped a towel sarong-wise about her body. She left a minor flood in the bathroom as she searched the floor there before retracing her footsteps into the bedroom. It was nowhere to be found.

'I knocked,' Ethan said as he appeared through the interconnecting door. It was the first time he'd used the door, and he knew it was ridiculous but he felt like an intruder in his own home. He didn't see Hannah at first, and then he spotted her small figure crouched beside the dressing table, silent tears pouring down her cheeks. The obvious conclusion to draw from such grief was that she hadn't told him everything that had happened. As he anticipated the worst his face darkened.

'I've lost my ring!' she wailed as she caught sight of him.

'What ring?' he asked blankly, moving to her side.

'My wedding ring.'

He felt relief. 'Is that all?' he said dismissively.

She hardly seemed to hear him. 'It might be in the kitchen, or on the stairs. I'll go and check.' She got rapidly to her feet—too rapidly, as it happened.

'You'll do nothing of the sort,' he said, catching hold of her elbows from behind and half lifting her across the room as her knees folded.

With a soft grunt he transferred her into his arms. She

was incredibly light. Was she naturally slender, or were there more surprises in store for him in the form of eating disorders? Nothing would surprise him after tonight!

'The ring doesn't matter; I can buy you a new one. You're overwrought!' The last sounded almost like an accusation.

Hannah sniffed as he placed her on her bed. Of course he could; why on earth had she reacted like that? Why should a ring that symbolised their marriage of convenience be precious to her? She must be more careful. He was probably suspecting he was married to a madwoman, she surmised, fairly accurately.

'Sorry,' she whispered huskily.

'You've had a bad night.' Her tears made him uncomfortable. It occurred to him that he hadn't seen this much of his wife before—even on the beach that summer she'd worn a baggy tee shirt over her swimming costume, and not even the children's pleas could make her enter the water.

The towel she wore cut across the high swell of her small breasts and ended... Her legs were quite long in proportion to her diminutive frame. His wandering gaze encountered a pair of solemn hazel eyes, watching him watching, and he looked away abruptly.

'I fetched this for the scratches.' He held out a tube of antiseptic cream.

'That's kind of you, Ethan.'

'Your back is badly scratched,' he observed.

'I can't see.'

'Or reach,' he pointed out practically. 'I expect you'll feel it tomorrow—there are some nasty bruises coming out. Are you covered for tetanus?'

'I think so.'

'"Think so" isn't sufficient; you must go to the surgery first thing in the morning for a booster. Turn around and I'll put some cream on your back.'

His touch was impersonal, firm, but gentle. She felt warm and relaxed, and—for the first time since she'd leapt from the moving vehicle—safe.

'You'll have to loosen this,' he said, pulling at the edge of the towel. The warm glow that had enveloped her was abruptly dispelled by a flurry of irrational anxiety.

'No, that's fine.'

'I'll probably be able to restrain myself at the sight of your flesh,' he observed drily.

'I didn't think that...' Her instinctive rejection of a more intimate touch had been no reflection on Ethan's intentions and she was mortified at the conclusion he'd drawn. She knew he didn't find her attractive. Even so, his next words did hurt.

'You're too thin.'

'I know.' In her teens she'd fantasised about waking up one morning and finding her awkward angles had been transformed into lissome curves. Now she knew better.

'Do you eat?'

'You know I do—' She stopped. In actual fact, it was rare that they ate together, only socially on the occasions they dined out together or had guests. Normally she ate with the children and Ethan ate alone later. He commuted to the City, and being a successful barrister seemed to keep him away from home a lot. He was tipped to be the next head of chambers when Sir James retired next year—the youngest in the chambers' long history.

Actually she didn't mind these absences; she was a lot more comfortable when he wasn't there—not that she found his company oppressive, exactly. She was always acutely conscious in his company of her deficiencies. When he looked at her she was always sure he was comparing her unfavourably with his first wife As always, the thought of the sainted Catherine made her wince.

'Mrs Turner will confirm the fact I could probably eat you under the table.' He wouldn't consider the children impartial witnesses—they doted on her—but the housekeeper was another matter.

'I've only ever seen you pick at your food. That's it.' He pulled up the towel. 'They're not deep; you won't scar.'

Should she tell him she was usually so nervous of making a social *faux pas* on the occasions he referred to that she couldn't stomach anything? On reflection she decided not to. Inadequacies—at least, hers—made Ethan impatient.

'I think that under the circumstances these French classes aren't such a good idea,' he mused slowly.

His words filled her with deep dismay and the first stirrings of rebellion. 'But Thursday is my night off, Ethan.'

'Night off?' he repeated coldly. 'You're not the nanny now, Hannah. You're my wife.'

'Of course I still work for you, Ethan. I just call you Ethan, not Mr Kemp.' And that had taken some getting used to! 'The contract's more permanent, and less flexible,' she added thoughtfully. 'That's all.'

He couldn't have looked more astounded if she'd popped him one on the nose. He breathed in sharply and the slab of his belly muscles became more noticeably concave. Hannah had heard girls on the beach in Nice commenting on his 'great pecs'; these too were visible, because even though he'd slipped on a blue top that matched his trousers he hadn't bothered to fasten it. She was no expert, but she didn't think their enthusiasm for his body had been misplaced.

'There is no need to think of yourself in that way,' he said, his colour heightened.

'Then as your wife I don't necessarily have to take your...advice.' Advice had a more tactful ring than order.

A combative light had entered his grey eyes. Possibly it was due to the unusual events of the evening, but Hannah found the circumstance more exhilarating than alarming.

'Perhaps you should consider your track record in the decision-making arena before throwing my advice back in my face.'

'Did you have a particular decision in mind?'

Despite the fact that she had remained meticulously polite, there was no mistaking the obstinate set of her rounded jaw. He viewed said jaw with serious misgivings.

'Getting into a car with a perfect stranger? Only a complete idiot would do anything so grossly irresponsible,' he said scornfully. 'Emma, at seven, would have more sense.'

She'd been stupid to imagine she could win an argument with Ethan. 'You wouldn't say that if I was a man,' she complained belligerently.

He blinked: she was pouting, actually pouting—Hannah! The sight of her rather full pink lips had the most unexpected effect on his body. 'Well, you're not a man,' he snapped. 'And in that outfit it's patently obvious.'

Hannah went bright pink and, after a furtive glance down at her body, began to tug the towel higher, but the material would only stretch just so far.

'I'm sorry if my skinny body offends you, but I didn't invite you into my room.' Even a fluffy bunny rabbit could get aggressive if you backed it into a corner, and she wasn't actually as weak and pliable as Ethan thought.

Early on she'd decided confrontation wasn't her style, but to survive ten years relatively unscathed after her spells in assorted foster homes, interspersed by the inevitable return to the children's home, wasn't the sign of a weak character. It wasn't an advantage in life to be brought up in care, but Hannah had never allowed herself to grow bitter, just as she'd never allowed herself to be influenced by the less savoury influences she had been surrounded by.

'I'll keep that in mind in the future,' he observed stiffly.

'I didn't mean…' She gave a sigh of frustration. 'The French classes mean a lot to me,' she admitted.

'Very obviously,' he drawled. With growing dismay she observed the pinched look around his nostrils.

It had been a waste of time appealing to his softer nature! 'I need to get away, be…I don't know—*me*!'

'Does that usually involve removing your wedding ring?'

Hannah could only stare at him in astonishment. He couldn't actually believe… 'I lost my ring.' It had always been too big; if she hadn't hated asking him for anything, she'd have told him so.

'You seem awfully passionate about a night-class.'

His faint condescending sneer really made her see red. 'Just a *class* to you!' she yelled. 'But then you have dozens of friends. You go out every day and meet people. I see the children—' And, as much as she loved Emma and Tom, the children weren't always enough. She broke off, breathing hard. Though one part of her felt appalled at her outburst, another part—a small part—felt relief.

'We have an active social life. My friends...'

'*Your* friends despise me. They only put up with me because I'm your appendage. Actually—' she smiled briefly, amazed at her daring '—I don't much like them, at least not most of them.'

The colour that suffused the pale, perfect oval of her small face was quite becoming. 'Colourless' was the adjective he most frequently associated with this girl he'd married—it sure as hell wasn't applicable now!

'Then why haven't you seen fit to mention it before?'

'I didn't think it was relevant. I'm quite prepared to take the rough with the smooth.' But I won't give up the French classes. It wasn't necessary to add this; Ethan wasn't dense.

'That's very tolerant of you. Do you consider there to have been much that is *rough* for you to endure over the past year?'

'Next you'll be saying I was in the gutter when you found me,' she cut in impatiently. She ignored his sharp inhalation of anger and continued firmly. 'You can expect my loyalty, but not my unstinting gratitude, Ethan. If you remember, I did warn you I wouldn't be the world's best hostess, but I'm a good mother.'

'Mother substitute.' She flinched, and his expression seemed to indicate he regretted his hasty response. 'The children love you.' This was meant to soften his sharp correction but only served to bring a lump of emotion to Hannah's throat. 'Do you find me such an ungenerous husband?'

It wasn't fair of him to bring affection into the discussion because affection, or rather the lack of it, had been implicit in their bargain.

'I didn't say that.'

Right from the outset he'd insisted that she spent money from the generous personal allowance that appeared in her bank account every month. Ethan Kemp's wife couldn't have a wardrobe that consisted of jeans and jumpers. When he'd discovered she couldn't overcome her reluctance to spend money, he'd sought the help of the wife of one of his colleagues.

Hannah wasn't sure whether Alice Chambers had genuinely awful taste or she just didn't like her. Whichever was the truth, the clothes Hannah came home with from their joint shopping expedition did nothing whatever for her slight figure, and the colours made her appear washed out and insipid.

Some of the annoyance faded from Ethan's expression as he took in the pale fragility of her unhappy face. With her glossy hair hanging softly about her face she looked incredibly young. She *was* incredibly young; he was apt to overlook the age gap sometimes. Usually she had the composure of someone much older.

'No, you didn't, but it is fairly obvious you're discontented. I had no idea.'

'How could you?' The retort escaped before she could censor it. Some days they barely exchanged two words. 'I'm not discontent, just tired,' she said dully. The loneliness of her position rushed in on her and it was more than she could bear tonight. Just go, please go! she thought miserably.

As if he detected her passionate wish, he turned abruptly. 'We'll talk in the morning.'

Now there's something to look forward to, she thought, torn between tears and laughter as the door closed. In the privacy of her secret dreams she'd imagined him using that door. Usually he'd just woken up to the fact that he'd been unaccountably blind to her charms. In none of those meticulously constructed scenarios had she had a runny nose, scratches over half her body or hair flopping in her eyes.

Falling in love with Ethan Kemp was the only truly spontaneous thing she could recall doing in her life. You didn't have to be a starry-eyed believer in love at first sight to have it happen to you; she was the living proof. Her prosaic soul had been set alight the instant she'd set eyes on him. He was tall, with an impressive athletic build, and one glance into those shrewd eyes had told her he had an intellect to match his muscles. Never one to respond to superficial beauty, she'd been inexplicably bowled over. None of these passionate cravings had been evident in her colourless replies as she'd sat through the interview. If they had she doubted she'd have got the job.

Worshipping him from afar had always made her particularly inarticulate in his presence, but, so long as the children were happy, Ethan's interest in their nanny had been minimal. When he'd first started to show an interest in her lukewarm friendship with Matt Carter, a local primary school teacher, she had almost allowed herself to think he might have noticed her as a person.

As it had turned out, he'd just been afraid history was about to repeat itself. Emma and Tom had had three nannies in the year before she'd arrived. Tom had been one, and he'd simply responded to anyone who'd offered him love and warmth. His sister had been a different proposition—five when Hannah had first arrived, and it had been an uphill battle for Hannah to win her trust. Her short life had taught Emma it was painful to love someone only to have them vanish. Hannah could identify with her suspicion, and slowly she'd won the child's trust, until by the end of that first year she'd become an integral part of the children's lives.

An indispensable part, as far as Ethan was concerned. They were now confident, happy children, and he'd been prepared to go to extraordinary lengths to provide them with continuing stability. He'd been shocked to recognise the possibility that Hannah might just follow the example of the previous three nannies and do something inconvenient like fall in love or get pregnant. He didn't actually *want* a wife, and, just in case Hannah had any doubts on the subject, he'd told her so.

He'd known her history when he'd offered her a home and financial security. No doubt he'd considered the bait irresistible to someone who was completely alone in the world. She'd never have to budget her meagre resources again; she'd have the family she'd always dreamed of— in short it was a fairy tale. The *but* was inescapable: he would never view her as anything other than a paid employee, no matter what her title. The pre-nuptial agreement he'd had her sign prior to the wedding had only served to reinforce this fact.

He had probably congratulated himself on his subtle, but clever presentation of the package when she'd appeared the next morning, looking unusually pale and subdued, and said the all-important 'yes'. He wouldn't have looked so happy if he'd suspected that, no matter how tempting his offer might appear to a girl who longed for roots and stability, it was love that had been the vital ingredient in the equation. Love that had made her ignore the logical part of her brain that told her that such a union could only give her pain.

CHAPTER TWO

TOM usually woke Hannah by creeping into her bed, often before six in the morning. This morning there was no solid little body against hers when she awoke. A light sleeper, she didn't normally need to set her alarm clock, but there had been nothing *normal* about the previous night! A whistle-stop, vaguely panicky tour revealed the children weren't in their rooms.

'Why didn't anyone wake me?' Hannah demanded breathlessly as she ran into the kitchen still tying the belt on her robe. 'Ouf, sorry,' she gasped as she rushed full tilt into her husband.

'I told them not to,' Ethan replied calmly.

She was conscious of the intimate contact of their bodies only for a few seconds before he solicitously steadied her and stepped away. It was enough to send her pulse-rate hammering. Although he didn't douse himself in masculine cologne, she could have recognised his presence blindfolded in any room. Her nostrils automatically flared as she got a full dose of his signature male fragrance.

'What are you doing here?' She instantly wished the words unsaid. Ethan didn't want or need her interest, and any suggestion of interrogation would be met with a sharp rebuttal. Now was the time to get their relationship back on its neatly designed unchallenging lines. Last night had been a blip in normality not a new chapter.

One dark brow quirked. 'I live here, remember.'

His dry tone brought a flush to her cheeks. 'Shouldn't you be in work?' *There I go again.*

As she spoke Hannah was conscious of the fact that they weren't alone; despite appearances, at least one pair of ears was undoubtedly taking in every word. The housekeeper had never made any comment on her employer's odd choice of bride, but she wouldn't have been human if the situation hadn't intrigued her.

Hannah sometimes wondered what she said about them to her husband when she returned home in the evenings. She'd been *in situ* when the first Mrs Kemp had been alive, and Hannah had half expected her to keep the sort of suspicious, unfriendly distance many of Ethan's friends did. To her relief this hadn't been the case. So long as Hannah didn't trespass on her domestic territory, she seemed perfectly at ease with the arrangement.

Ethan didn't normally participate in the usual morning chaos of dressing and feeding the children, then ferrying Emma to school. He was generally leaving the house as Hannah fetched the children downstairs. He appeared to start the day with nothing more substantial than a cup of strong black coffee, a practice Hannah privately had serious reservations about. She had never voiced her concerns, because Ethan's welfare was one of those things that were out of bounds. She had no doubt that with a few well-chosen words he could and would subdue any pretensions she had in that direction.

'Not this morning, Hannah. Dear God,' he murmured, inspecting the streak of strawberry jam he'd just discovered down the sleeve of his dark jacket with a grimace. 'How does he manage to spread it that far?' he wondered, casting a fascinated look in the direction of his chubby-faced son, who smiled back with cherubic innocence from his highchair.

'I want down!' he announced, banging his spoon on the plastic table-top.

'Soon, Tom,' Hannah responded automatically. She pushed her hair behind her ears and tried to work out what Ethan was doing here. A devoted father he might be, but he'd never involved himself in the more mundane of parental duties. 'You should have woken me. I'll be late getting Emma to school.'

'Daddy's taking me, Mummy.'

The 'Mummy' was a new thing, and it still gave Hannah a glow of pleasure to hear it. Ethan had never commented on her promotion from 'Hannah' in his daughter's eyes, but she was sure he didn't like it. His restraint only reminded her that from his point of view her role within the household would always be one of necessity rather than desire.

'*You are?*' she gasped, unable to hide her surprise.

'You consider the task too complex for me?'

'You just sit down, my dear, and I'll get you a nice cup of tea. Mr Kemp has told me about the nasty accident you were in. What you need is a rest,' the housekeeper advised.

Hannah's eyes flew to Ethan's face as her hand went automatically to her scratched cheek. So that was to be the story, she thought philosophically. It certainly made her appear less foolish than the truth.

'I feel fine—just a little stiff, Mrs Turner.'

'I want out, now!' Patience was uncharted territory for a three-year-old.

Hannah unclipped his harness and heaved his sleep-suit-clad body into her arms. His sturdy frame made her conscious of bruises she hadn't known she had. She wasn't able totally to subdue the wince.

'Give him to me,' Ethan said, holding his arms out.

'I'm fine.'

'Martyrdom is an overrated and tedious virtue,' Ethan observed in a bored drawl.

Hannah handed over her charge with as much dignity as she could muster. Normally their parental duties were strictly, if unofficially, defined, and it was vaguely disorientating to have her role so thoroughly usurped.

Ethan might well regret his chivalry when he discovered that the wet kiss his beaming son had pressed somewhere east of his mouth had left a blob of porridge adhering to his freshly shaved cheek. A wicked impulse made her keep this information to herself.

'Will you do my hair?' Emma slid onto Hannah's knee and solemnly passed her a comb and ribbons.

'With your permission?' She shot Ethan a challenging look. She sounded cranky and didn't much care. She knew he was watching her again and it made her feel uncomfortable.

'I'd say that constitutes light duties,' he conceded. Whilst playing a tickling game, which Hannah thought might well result in his small son throwing up, he watched Hannah's expert fingers twist Emma's fluffy golden locks into the desired design. Emma was a beautiful child who looked remarkably like a miniature version of her mother. Hannah was sure Ethan didn't need the constant reminder to keep Catherine's memory fresh—several people had lost no time telling Hannah how passionately in love he'd been, how he'd worshipped her.

Hannah had been astounded the first time she'd seen Ethan with his children. Who would have guessed that behind the austere, rather daunting façade there lurked such a warm and humorous man? She'd thought his attitude towards her might bend a little over the months, but he'd never actually dropped the formality with her. She'd never been in any danger of forgetting her position in this household.

It wouldn't be long before Emma at least began to notice that her parents weren't like other people's: no hugs or teasing, no shared history of private jokes. Ethan didn't appear to have taken this aspect into account in his calculations. Children were sharp; nothing much escaped their observant eyes. It would be interesting, and probably uncomfortable, Hannah reflected, to see how he dealt with the inevitable questions.

'I'll be back shortly,' he said as he stood, the open doorway framing the sight of daughter and father hand in hand.

'Work...?' she faltered.

'I've cancelled my appointments for this morning. Cal Morgan will see you at ten. I'll take you to the surgery— for that tetanus jab,' he added as she stared at him blankly.

'Quite right, you can't be too careful,' the housekeeper observed approvingly. 'Tom will be just fine with me. I'll take him for his bath, won't I, darling? Kiss for Mummy.'

When Hannah emerged from the grubby embrace Ethan had gone. This new personal interest in her welfare obviously stemmed from his opinion that she wasn't capable of taking care of herself. It was frustrating to realise that she had nobody to blame for the situation but herself. If only he hadn't caught her last night. It had been an inconvenient time to discover the man she'd married was either an insomniac or a secret drinker, possibly both. The idea brought a whimsical smile to her lips. She couldn't imagine Ethan indulging in weaknesses of any variety!

She'd just have to reestablish herself in his eyes as being more than capable of taking care of herself. Driving herself to the doctor's surgery was step one of this process. He'd be glad to be relieved of this tedious chore.

That view took on a rapid sea change when she emerged from the surgery to find Ethan standing beside her Volvo. His long fingers were rapping an impatient tune on the bonnet. He appeared to be muttering under his breath at regular intervals. He straightened up at the sound of her feet crunching on the gravel. His dark brows met over the bridge of his nose as he recognised her.

'What the hell are you playing at?'

Whilst his attitude to her lacked warmth, she couldn't remember any occasion when his manner towards her hadn't been faultlessly polite. The flash of anger in his grey eyes and the unmistakable message his whole body language was shouting threw her totally off balance. What had she done?

'I'm not playing at anything, Ethan.'

'Don't waste that "butter wouldn't melt in your mouth" look on me, Hannah Smith… It won't wash any more.'

'Kemp, I'm Hannah Kemp.' He might like to pretend this weren't true sometimes, but it was.

He rubbed a hand through his dark hair, disrupting the sleek silhouette. 'You were less trouble as Smith,' he reflected after a thoughtful pause. 'I offered to drive you because you're very obviously not fit to sit behind a wheel. What are you trying to do—smash the parts you missed last night?'

'That's a ridiculous overstatement!' she protested. 'And don't think you're the only one regretting this marriage,' she yelled wildly.

His expression hardened into one of icy disdain as his cold glance whipped up and down her slender figure. Under the scrutiny she forced herself to straighten up, even though the ache in her ribs intensified.

'Marriage to me is one of those decisions you'd better learn to live with.' The unspoken 'or else' was clearly there in capital letters.

'Save your intimidation for the courtroom,' she told him with uncharacteristic steel.

'I'd never make that mistake—strong-arm tactics with someone who looks as vulnerable and fragile as you do right now would lose me the jury's sympathy.'

'I didn't mean to wound your professional pride.'

Her sarcastic murmur sent his dark brows towards his hairline. 'Happily we're not in the courtroom right now, so I'll continue to behave like a bully—you're obviously very at home with that image of me,' he observed tautly. 'Have you seen the way you're moving, woman? It's obvious every step hurts.'

She grimaced—that was almost exactly what Cal had said before he'd insisted on examining her. She gazed at her husband resentfully. 'My ribs are bruised, not broken, and Cal has given me a prescription for some painkillers.'

'Well, the next time you decide to get in a car with a maniac try and remember you're a mother, not a bloody stunt woman!'

Anyone would think she'd done this for the sole purpose of inconveniencing him! Ethan could be mind-bogglingly selfish at times.

'Don't worry, I don't need a nursemaid. You don't have to waste your time at home for my sake.'

'Nursemaid!' he scoffed. 'I'm beginning to think you need a minder. As for staying at home, I'm in court this afternoon. Alexa has agreed to pick Emma up from school.'

Hannah didn't have time to hide her dismay from him.

'I do think you might make a little bit more effort with Alexa—she is the children's grandmother.'

Effort, me? thought Hannah. She grated her teeth at the sheer injustice of this criticism. Alexa Harding had been horrified when she'd learnt that the nanny was to take her daughter's place. Having any woman take Catherine's place would have been hard for her to accept, but the fact that Hannah was, in her eyes, menial household help made the situation unacceptable to the older woman.

At first Hannah had thought she might come round, if she saw the children were happy, but, if anything, the closer Hannah had become to the children, the more bitter their grandmother had become. She never missed an opportunity to belittle Hannah in front of Ethan—she was about as subtle as dripping acid. Hannah longed for Ethan to side with her—*just once*. Only he never did. He remained aloof from the petty squabbles.

'It's very kind of her,' Hannah said in a expressionless voice. Anxiety crowded out the appearance of calm as she rushed on. 'You didn't tell her what actually happened, did you?' Alexa would have a field-day with that sort of information.

'Does it matter?'

Hannah grabbed his wrist, her fingers digging into his skin. 'Yes, it does,' she persisted urgently.

Ethan looked from her pale fingers to her flushed face with a quizzical expression. 'I stuck to the accident story.'

Hannah heaved a sigh of relief. 'Thank you.' Realising she was still clinging, she abruptly released her grip.

'The truth isn't the sort of story I'm likely to spread around.'

'Are you trying to imply that by getting into his car I was inviting...?'

'My God, don't be so touchy!' he exploded. 'I'm not implying anything of the sort. Hopefully you've learnt something from the experience, but that might be asking too much.'

Didn't he ever make a mistake? 'I've learnt not to expect any sympathy from you.' She flushed at the implication that she desired sympathy from him.

'Not when you act like a naïve schoolgirl,' he snapped back crisply. 'Get in the car. Not this one—mine,' he added as she reached for her car keys. 'No, don't put those away,' he said, catching her hand. 'You'd better lock it first. Do you make a habit of leaving a welcome card for car thieves?'

'I thought I had locked it. I *always* lock it.' His sceptical sneer made her want to scream.

Ethan drove a high-powered black BMW. He parked at the end of a tree-lined avenue and told her tersely he'd only be ten minutes. He didn't explain where he was going, but then he never did. Whatever his business was, he looked pretty grim.

Ethan was always punctual, and it was barely ten

minutes later that he returned. He opened the door and threw in her brown leather shoulder bag.

'I thought you'd like this back. You'd better check everything is there,' he advised, sliding into the driver's seat. 'It won't bite; you take a look.'

'Where did you get it?' she asked hoarsely.

The engine purred into life. 'Where do you think?'

'How do you know where he lives? What did you do...?'

'The college was very helpful when I explained good old Craig had left his wallet in my car last night. Shocking security,' he observed mildly.

'What did he say? Did he just hand it over?'

'He said too much,' Ethan observed curtly.

'About me?' she asked miserably. She could just imagine what sordid lies he'd wheeled out to justify his actions. She felt sick just imagining that Ethan had believed any of it. She couldn't bring herself to look at him.

'Don't worry, he admitted the truth eventually.'

'Eventually?' She looked at his grim, hard-edged profile and realised she was being pretty slow. Ethan wasn't the sort of man people intimidated, but he was more than capable of doing the intimidating if he felt the situation justified it. His next words confirmed her dawning suspicions.

'Craig is now personally acquainted with fear. That was what you wanted, wasn't it? I forget how long you had in mind, but I always think it's quality not quantity that counts.'

His thin-lipped smile made her shudder. This wasn't the indulgent father; this was a ruthless man—a dangerous man. She'd never actually appreciated before just how daunting Ethan could be.

'You didn't...didn't hit him, did you?'

His charcoal-grey suit was pristine and his silk tie lay smoothly against the white background of his shirt. He didn't look like a man who'd just been brawling. Her eyes went to his knuckles as his hands lay lightly on the steering wheel—no tell-tale marks.

'Nothing so crude. I just told him what I'd do to him if he ever touched you or any other woman again.'

'And that scared him?'

'You had to be there.' His smile was savagely silky. It made Hannah shudder. It made her realise how little she knew this man she'd married.

'Are lawyers supposed to behave like that?' she asked doubtfully.

'I didn't go in there wearing my wig, Hannah. I went in there as your husband. I didn't lay a finger on him— of course, if he'd tried...' He shook his head rather regretfully. 'I knew he'd cave in. I've seen his type often enough—inadequate bullies.' His grey eyes were filled with contempt as he flicked her a sideways glance. Happily the contempt was intended for the loathsome Craig.

She looked away and pretended to go through the contents of her bag. 'It's all here,' she said, not actually registering what was before her eyes. The words 'as your husband' kept going through her mind. The warm glow was a ludicrous response; she knew he hadn't meant anything by it. All the same...

'Aren't you stopping for lunch?' she asked, trying to sound as if it didn't matter one way or the other. She'd had a lot of experience; she could hear what sounded like authentic lack of interest in her voice.

'I'm meeting Miranda. She's assisting me this afternoon.'

Miranda, the newest recruit to Ethan's chambers, was everything Hannah would have liked to be. Not only was she beautiful, she had brains which had earned her respect in a male-dominated world.

Hannah often wondered if Miranda was the reason Ethan didn't get home until so late—suspiciously late on Friday nights. It wasn't really reasonable to suppose he remained celibate; he was a virile, attractive—*very* attractive—man. Even if he was still hopelessly in love with Catherine, he was still human. She knew he'd always be discreet; it wasn't in his nature to humiliate her by flaunting his affairs. All the same, the thought of him with the beautiful redhead tortured her.

'That's nice.'

'Is it?'

'I wouldn't know,' she said in an exasperated tone. 'I was just being polite.' She tried to slip back into their old relationship, and the only thanks she got were his snide comments. There was no pleasing some people.

'Now I know why I married you—for your lovely manners.'

What she'd done to deserve his mockery she didn't know. She'd grown accustomed to his indifference over the past year, his occasional irritation, but he actually looked as though he disliked her this morning.

'No, you married me because you wanted a low-maintenance wife who would make as little impact as possible on your life!' The resentment bubbled up and overflowed into these unwise observations before she could stop it.

He flinched as the accuracy of her husky accusation hit him. 'Well, I'd hardly call your antics over the last twenty-four hours low maintenance.' The unvarnished truth sliced uncomfortably through his rationalisations, and, not unnaturally, made him as mad as hell.

Ethan had managed to convince himself that his motives in marrying Hannah, whilst not being totally altruistic, hadn't been completely selfish. She'd had so little and he'd been offering her a standard of living that she could never have aspired to. It was a sound business arrangement. She'd always given the impression of being content. Her affection for the children was indisputable, as was theirs for her.

Until he'd been faced with the prospect of losing her, he hadn't realised how much this quiet girl had become part of the household. The part that had given it the first breath of normality and stability in a long time. It was incredible how someone so unobtrusive could make such a difference. Unobtrusive? Looking at the angry belligerence that tightened the soft contours of her face, he decided the label seemed singularly inappropriate.

'If I'd had my way you wouldn't have known at all about last night. It's your fault for being an insomniac!'

'Wouldn't have known!' He seized on the words as if they were a guilty admission. 'I thought as much— how many other *secrets* do you keep from me?'

'Secrets, *me*?' The idea was laughable. 'If I told you everything I do in a day I'd bore your socks off.' Not like the lovely Miranda, she thought. I bet he hangs on her every syllable.

The guilt he felt at the most unexpected moments came rushing in and his voice was harsh. 'So your life's drudgery, is it?'

'Luxurious drudgery,' she corrected sarcastically, her outstretched arms encompassing the elegant surroundings of the period-furnished drawing room. A room that was a tribute to the good taste of her predecessor. 'What more could a girl ask for? And you accuse me of being touchy!' she snorted.

He regarded her delicately flushed face, flashing eyes and mutinously set mouth with an odd expression. His stillness made Hannah lick her lips nervously.

Unexpectedly, he caught her chin in one hand. 'What's happened to you? You're not the same person.' Everything had been going so well. Why the hell did she have to start acting like a woman all of a sudden? And, even worse, why was he thinking of her as a woman?

'Perhaps you've confused silence with lack of feelings, Ethan. I do *feel*.'

'And what feelings arouse your passions?' he wondered out loud. His eyes dropped to the rapid rise and fall of her small, high breasts, and a look she'd never seen before slid into his eyes.

'Things,' she replied huskily.

'Like French classes.' A trace of discontent had entered his voice.

'Like French classes,' she agreed.

'Perhaps it would be safer for you to look closer to home to satisfy your passions.' His thumb moved in a circular motion over the small, rounded chin.

'Do you speak French, Ethan?'

'It wasn't the search for intellectual stimulation that made you do a dangerous thing like get in that car last night. The man turned out to be an idiot, but what if he'd had a more subtle approach? Would a furtive kiss in the dark have been so unacceptable to you, Hannah? Isn't that what you secretly wanted?'

She tore her face from his grip. 'The only person I'd like less to be touched by than Craig...is you!' The insulting picture of herself as some sexually frustrated female desperate for male attention made her blood boil. Ironically, the only male attention she craved was his. At least he couldn't taunt her with the truth.

'Brave words.'

A logical assessment later would tell her she'd backed his male ego into a corner and the outcome had been a foregone conclusion. Logic didn't come to her assistance at the time.

It was nothing like her imaginary kisses. Imagination didn't have texture and warmth and taste. 'Melting' had been a word before; now it was a reality as her body dissolved in a rush of mind-numbing sensual delight. Her lips automatically parted under the imprint of his mouth. The taste of him glutted her senses.

When it stopped her disorientation was total. She felt numb and strangely dizzy. She touched the back of her hand to her parted, slightly swollen lips. The eyes she raised to his face were still clouded with a misty languor. It afforded Hannah a tiny measure of satisfaction that Ethan looked to be equally stunned by his actions.

Over the years Hannah had formulated a vague theory that for women it was easy to stop kissing—it was only men who were driven beyond sense and reason by such an essentially innocent pastime.

Innocent! Oh, dear, it looked as if she'd have to re-evaluate her hypothesis. Limited research was obviously to blame for her inaccurate conclusions.

'That was childish of me.' He was slipping back into his cool professional persona with insulting ease. An adjustment to his gold cufflinks, a judicious twitch of the tasteful tie.

'*Childish* isn't the first word that springs to my mind,' she returned huskily. The destructive friction of his skilful lips and wicked tongue had filled her with an entirely adult ache. It began low in the pit of her belly, but spread just about everywhere.

'I suppose you expect me to apologise.' From the stubborn, closed expression on his face, she concluded this was unlikely.

'Why? I liked it.'

'Dear God!' he grated, his stance growing more rigid as he discovered she was examining his lips with dreamy curiosity.

The sharp exclamation brought Hannah belatedly to her senses. She bit hard on her criminally indiscreet tongue and felt the hot colour wash up her neck until her face was aflame.

'I mean, a kiss is just…'

'A kiss?' he suggested.

'Exactly,' she said, relief making her go a bit overboard on the enthusiasm. 'I don't think we should mention…'

'You liked it.'

Hannah frowned, not trusting his suddenly innocent expression. 'Your loss of control.'

'That's very generous of you.' Perversely, he found himself vaguely dissatisfied that she was suggesting what he had wanted only seconds before.

When the doorbell rang later that afternoon Hannah squared her shoulders and steeled herself for a dose of Alexa. She glanced at the clock on the mantel and frowned—she was early. Hannah was sitting cross-legged on the carpet, playing with Tom, and she smiled wryly as she pulled the child onto her lap, aware she was using him almost as a shield against the battery of criticism she knew was about to be lobbed at her head.

'Mrs Kemp, it's a Mr Dubois.'

'Jean-Paul!' Hannah exclaimed in pleasure as the figure behind Mrs Turner stepped forward.

'Hannah, forgive the intrusion.'

'It's no intrusion—come in. Would you like tea, coffee?'

'Coffee would be nice.'

'Would you mind, Mrs Turner?' She smiled at the housekeeper. 'Sit down, please.' She couldn't understand what her night-class tutor was doing here, but, having stealed herself to face the dreaded Alexa, it was marvellous to see a friendly face. You're a coward, Hannah, she told herself angrily. Show a bit more backbone!

Jean-Paul Dubois settled himself in an armchair and looked admiringly around the room. Hannah saw his glance dwell on a framed picture of Ethan with Catherine: two beautiful people, the perfect couple. He was too polite to comment.

'You have a lovely home.' He pushed his wire-framed glasses up the bridge of his nose. They were the only vaguely intellectual thing about the young Frenchman's appearance. He looked more like a male model than a university lecturer, which was his daytime job.

'Home' had an optimistically permanent ring to it. 'It's been in my husband's family for a long time.' Ethan had inherited the place years ago from his father, and though his mother had first stayed on in her marital home she had left shortly after Ethan's first marriage. Hannah had only met Faith Kemp once, at their own wedding, and the lady hadn't bothered hiding her disapproval of the match. Hannah had heard with her own ears Faith read a scalding lecture to her son on the subject.

'He is a beautiful *bébé*,' Jean-Paul, said, laughing as Tom lobbed a pink elephant at his head.

'Thank you.'

Jean-Paul nodded at the question in her eyes. 'You are wondering why I am here?'

'It's very nice to see you.'

'You are a very talented student. Some people have a natural talent for languages—you are one of them.'

Hannah flushed with pleasure. She'd certainly enjoyed the classes, but she hadn't thought she was anything special. 'I've had a good teacher.'

'That's why I wish you'd reconsider your decision to leave the class. I know there are many pressures when you have a family... The unfortunate accident—'

'Stop right there,' Hannah said, holding up her hand. Tom wriggled off her knee and went over to Jean-Paul, who took the theft of his spectacles in good part. 'What makes you think I'm leaving the class? How did you know I'd had an...accident?' She flushed a little as she said this.

'Your husband spoke to me earlier,' he explained.

Hannah drew a wrathful breath. 'He did, did he?' she said quietly, with a brilliantly false smile.

'I did tell him how sorry I would be to see you go. I know our classes are light-hearted, but I was hoping you could go further.'

'Further?' she said, startled for a moment from her contemplation of a suitable punishment for her overbearing husband. So long as she made the children happy, he had no right to interfere so blatantly in her life. One night a week to herself wasn't too much to ask for.

'Have you ever thought of doing a degree?'

'Me?' Hannah shook her head. 'I couldn't do that—I've no formal schooling to speak of. I left school at sixteen.' That was when the State had stopped being responsible for her, and she'd woken up to the fact that taking care of herself and being in full-time education weren't compatible.

'Your family did not mind?'

'I had no family,' Hannah explained briefly. Her mouth tightened at the sympathetic light she saw in his eyes. She hated pity! 'I trained as a nursery nurse.' A job that gave her both an income and a roof over her head had seemed a practical compromise.

'I know you are very young, Hannah.'

'Twenty-three.'

'But you would still be classed as a mature candidate for university entrance. There is quite a lot of flexibility for the right candidates.'

'And you think I'm the right candidate?'

Jean-Paul smiled as he heard the hint of wistfulness creep into her voice. 'The perfect candidate. Some mature students find the finances a drain, but you...' His Gallic gesture took in the undoubted affluence of the surroundings.

'I don't know what to say.' Could she? Ethan would never agree. All the same, the idea did take hold. Over the years she'd seen people much less able than herself go to university. It had been something that had seemed always tantalisingly out of reach.

'Say yes, *chérie*.' Satisfied he'd presented his case, he didn't labour the point. 'Where, *bébé*, are my glasses? You must lead me by the hand, Hannah. I am blind.'

Laughing, Hannah reached under the sofa and retrieved the spectacles. Still on her knees at the foot of Jean-Paul's chair, she slid them obligingly back onto his nose.

At this point the door opened and the housekeeper returned, bearing a tray laden with coffee and scones. 'I put plenty on for everyone. I know how hungry Emma is when she comes home.'

'Can I have one now?' Emma skipped into the room beside the upright figure of her grandmother, whose pale blue eyes swept over the room with a look of malicious triumph. 'Can I, Mummy?'

'Get changed out of your uniform first,' Hannah said, pushing back the wing of silky hair that had flopped in her eyes. 'Hello, Alexa. It was good of you to pick Emma up.'

'Hannah, what a delightful surprise—I half expected you to be bed-bound, from the way Ethan was talking. You look glowing, my dear. Aren't you going to introduce me to your *friend*?'

Determined not to rise to the bait, Hannah simply nodded in Jean-Paul's direction. 'This is Jean-Paul Dubois, my French tutor. Jean-Paul, this is Alexa...'

Jean-Paul got to his feet and, clasping the older woman's hand lightly, raised it to his lips. '*Madame*. No, Hannah, do not get up—you are busy with your family. Will you think about what I said?'

Hannah couldn't help wincing as she got to her feet. The painkillers had improved the situation, but she was still stiff and sore. Gallant to his fingertips, Jean-Paul solicitously took her elbow.

'Thank you,' she murmured gratefully as she straightened up. 'It was good of you to call. Goodbye.'

'*Au revoir,*' he corrected.

'Does Ethan know you entertain your men whilst he is out working?' Alexa settled herself into the chair Jean-Paul had vacated. She was a handsome woman who had kept a youthful figure. The permanent lines of bitterness around her mouth robbed her of what otherwise would have been beauty.

'Man, Alexa,' Hannah corrected calmly. 'And I feel
sure I can rely on you to tell Ethan.' She was well aware
that it wouldn't occur to Ethan that a man like Jean-Paul
would find her attractive—that was part of the reason
he'd married her.

The older woman looked a little taken aback by her
composure. 'I expect you've been playing up a couple
of scratches for all it's worth. Catherine never let personal discomfort stop her doing what she wanted. She
wasn't afraid of anything!'

Which was why she wasn't here now! Hannah repressed this unworthy observation. Tom had been barely
a month old when Catherine had decided to ride in a
point-to-point. When her horse had gone lame she had
taken on a mount whose rider had been injured, even
though the animal was renowned for an unpredictable
temper. She had to have known the risk she was taking
when she'd ignored advice—it was only because of her
pregnancy that she'd missed out on a place in the British
Olympic team. Hannah wasn't in a position to speculate
about what drove someone like that; perhaps it was irrelevant. Whatever the motivation, the outcome had been
tragic.

'I'm not Catherine.'

Alexa's laugh was shrill. 'And I'm sure Ethan remem-
bers what he lost every time he looks at you,' she
sneered. 'Thomas, put that down!' she cried as the little
boy lifted a porcelain figure off the lower shelf of a
display case.

'Give it to Mummy, Tom,' Hannah said quietly, so as
not to alarm the child. 'Good boy,' she praised as he
handed it over. She placed the delicate ornament on a
higher shelf. Alexa's words wouldn't have hurt so much
if she hadn't known they were true. She could never

hope to compete with the vital, glowing creature Ethan had loved.

'That was one of Catherine's favourites.'

It would be, of course, Hannah thought philosophically. 'Well, it's safe now.'

'I don't know why you allow the children in this room. They ruin everything.'

Hannah sighed; they'd been through this before. 'This is a family home, Alexa, not a showcase. It's meant to be lived in.' The whole place was in danger of becoming a shrine. It was bad enough that almost every room was filled with photos of its late mistress; the trophies of her sporting achievements remained as a memorial to her talent and sense of adventure. Not only had she been a top-class horsewoman, she'd been an accomplished yachtswoman, and somewhere along the way she'd managed to pack in a spot of rock-climbing. She had obviously been one of those people who found danger attractive, even addictive. Her talent hadn't been limited to competing in the sporting world—she had founded and run a small manufacturing business which specialised in high-class sporting gear.

Hannah might not be able to alter the tastefully co-ordinated decor to suit her own taste, but she had been able to smuggle the odd toy box gradually into the drawing room and pin Emma's early attempts at art on the kitchen wall, despite Alexa's objections. A minor victory, but for Hannah a triumph. Children didn't need the stifling atmosphere of a museum.

'The place is looking positively shabby. I know Ethan doesn't like to entertain much now Catherine is gone, but...' Alexa's aristocratic nose wrinkled in disgust.

This was a patent untruth—all the main reception rooms had been redecorated a couple of months previously. The interior decorators had duplicated all the existing decor down to the smallest detail.

Emma's explosive return into the room spared Hannah Alexa's more obvious displays of dislike. She knew it went deeper than dislike. It sometimes felt as if the woman had made Hannah the focus for all her grief and anger over her daughter's death.

CHAPTER THREE

AFTER a year of marriage Ethan came knocking on Hannah's bedroom door for the second time in as many days. This time she heard him. It was Friday night and he was home late, as usual.

'This is getting to be habit-forming,' she said as he stepped into the room in response to her crisp invitation.

It was a line she'd been working on all evening, and she was quite pleased with her delivery. She might have been flustered to see him if Alexa's actions hadn't been so predictable. She'd known he'd appear at some point, demanding an explanation.

'You getting into trouble?' Elbow against the wall, he loosened his tie and looked at her in a distinctly un-friendly fashion.

In her innocence she'd imagined that with love off the menu she might settle for the closeness of a special friendship. Being ignored had been a lot easier to bear than his open dislike.

'Am I?' She didn't appear too bothered at the possi-bility, which she could see surprised him. She'd discov-ered a perverse pleasure in surprising him over the past day or so. It was satisfying, shaking him out of his iron certitude. It was only natural, she decided, to resent the person you loved when he didn't even notice you ex-isted—at least not in *that* way.

'I suppose you've received reports of me inviting my hordes of lovers to cavort on the Aubusson carpet in the

44

drawing room.' The mental image of bacchanalia brought a tiny smile to her lips.

'You don't seem to be taking this very seriously.' He ran a hand over the dark growth of stubble that shadowed his angular jaw.

'I'm only amazed that you are,' she fired back wearily. 'No, actually I'm not, because you don't have a very high opinion of me, do you, Ethan?'

She'd worked so damned hard to be what he wanted, but that had counted for nothing when she'd disrupted the smooth running of his life. One little slip, and he was looking at her as though she had something contagious. So her *little slip* had been spectacular—she hadn't asked him to get involved personally.

'You've always done what I've asked of you,' he observed noncommittally. Despite his words, she didn't detect any wholehearted endorsement in his slightly uncomfortable stance. He looked as though his wife's bedroom was the last place in the world he wanted to be. Anger was her best response to the pain this knowledge brought.

'You're just wondering what else I've done besides.'

'When the woman I married starts behaving like a teenager rebelling for the hell of it, I do start wondering—yes!' he agreed in a driven voice. 'You're acting completely out of character.'

'And you'd know all about my character?'

Her mockery brought an angry gleam to his narrowed eyes. 'I'm sorry if you didn't have the opportunity to get the rebellion out of your system when most of us do, but I've no desire whatever to become the focal point for your childish aggression. I don't feel even vaguely paternal towards you.' His lips twisted into a grimace of distaste.

'I wasn't looking for a father-figure when I married you!' Please, God, don't let him ask what I *was* looking for, she prayed, as she recognised the opening she'd given him. She needn't have been concerned—Ethan thought he knew all about her motivation.

'No, you were looking for security, which is understandable. Only now you're discovering that there's *more* to life than comfort. There's excitement.' Her fragile poise deserted her completely as his grey eyes raked her face. 'And sex.'

Her chest felt so tight she could hardly breathe. 'How dare you talk like that to me?'

'I *dare* because our lives here only work because we accept certain limitations,' he said brutally. 'It's a very delicate balance, and when you start flirting with French studs…'

'I expect Jean-Paul would find the stereotyping very flattering,' she breathed, furious that he could calmly taint an innocent friendship—God, it wasn't even that!— with his nasty innuendo! 'If you hadn't tried to run my life for me, Ethan, Jean-Paul wouldn't even have come here. You'll be relieved to hear it wasn't my body he was after,' she hissed sarcastically. 'But then I'm sure you didn't think that. You played safe when you picked me, didn't you?' she accused bitterly. 'You picked the plainest female you could find in the knowledge that, no matter how much you ignored me, there wasn't going to be anyone else queuing up to show me a good time!'

'If *Jean-Paul* wasn't here to show you "a good time"—' her face flamed as he quoted her heated words '—why did he come?'

'He wants me to do a degree—in French.'

He gave a short, hard laugh. 'It's more original than wanting to show you his etchings,' he conceded.

'Why do you assume it's a joke? You think I'm too stupid?' she asked from between gritted teeth.

'Well, you're not behaving like an intellectual giant right now, are you?'

'Is that a fact?' Forgetting her rather prim pose of crossed ankles and folded hands, she had deserted the chintz armchair and was pacing the room. 'How am I behaving, Ethan?'

'Over-emotionally, irrationally…'

'You, on the other hand, are the epitome of self-restraint and reason. Well, I've got news that you can file away in that rational brain of yours: not only will I *not* stop going to evening classes, I've every intention of exploring the possibility of taking it further.' If he hadn't pushed her she doubted she would have had the nerve seriously to explore the possibility. Ironically it was Ethan's scorn that had hardened her determination.

'I'm sure taking it further is exactly what Dubois had in mind,' he sneered. 'Only you're my wife!'

'My God, I hope for the sake of your clients you come up with more original arguments than that in court.'

'You can sneer, but you can't alter facts,' he countered, his face dark with anger.

He'd been inclined to dismiss Alexa's wild stories, and until he'd entered Hannah's room he'd expected to hear an adequate explanation. He'd been irritated at the necessity of confronting her after a long and tedious day, but nothing more.

Far from lulling his suspicions, her defiant attitude had made it clear she was capable of ruining their arrangement with her wilful behaviour. Her habitually calm hazel eyes had deepened to green as she glared at him before resuming her rhythmic barefooted tread of the deep-piled carpet.

He almost groaned out loud. A classic case of still waters running deep, only he didn't need, or require, deep. He needed shallow and efficient. He didn't want a glimpse of Hannah's passions; he wanted things back to normal. At the end of the day he could always come home knowing she would have coped with any household crises with quiet efficiency, his children would be happy and content and nobody would make any emotional demands on him. He hadn't realised how much he'd come to rely on this small oasis of peace until he'd been unexpectedly deprived of it.

'Some facts you can alter,' she said, coming to a dead halt with her back still to him. 'We could get a divorce—an annulment, even!' She spun around, her face alight with inspiration. 'It's not as if we have…' she shrugged '…you know.'

'Don't forget you signed the pre-nuptial—' My God, he thought, staring at her. She means it!

Her imperative gesture stopped him mid-flow. 'I don't care about that,' she said simply. All she cared about was getting out of this situation. Being married to a man she was crazy about, a man who thought of her as a sexless nonentity. She'd been mad to think she could cope; she'd been made to think it would lead down the path of her wishful thinking.

Ethan blinked, recalling the amount of money it had been agreed she would get if she stayed with him until Tom was sixteen. 'And the children?'

'That's the best part,' she told him enthusiastically, willing him to see the logic of her scheme. 'I could still look after the children. When Tom starts school I could go to university and still help with them. I wouldn't do anything to harm the children, Ethan.'

'So I'm the only part of this equation that you don't like?'

The desperate quality of her wild proposition said more about her unhappiness than anything else could have. The irony of the situation failed to amuse him. One of the reasons marriage to Hannah had been a good idea was that he'd wanted to put himself off-limits to all the women who, almost before the funeral was over, had made it obvious they were willing to offer him succour and comfort. His wife obviously found him easy to resist.

'You were a much nicer employer than husband,' she said fairly. 'And I've been an abysmal failure as a wife; admit it. I irritate you, embarrass you. I have appalling dress sense.'

'Appalling dress sense wasn't grounds for divorce the last time I looked.'

'But non-consummation is grounds for annulment.'

'So we're to annul our marriage and then you resume your job as nanny. Is that about the size of it?'

When he put it like that it didn't sound quite as feasible as it had when her feverish mind had seized on the solution. She nodded, but there was less certainty in her face now.

'Are you on some medication I don't know about?' he enquired with interest.

She sank down onto the edge of her bed with a sigh. 'Maybe I didn't think this through exactly. There's no need to be sarcastic. I was trying to help.'

'Then I hope you've put all thought of annulment out of your head. Unless both parties co-operate it's hell to prove unless you're a... Dear God,' he said slowly, staring at her averted face. 'You are, aren't you?' He sounded so profoundly shocked that in other circumstances she might have laughed.

'What if I am?' she responded belligerently. Being a virgin at the advanced age of twenty-three was certainly an embarrassment, and she was sensitive about the subject.

'It never occurred to me,' he admitted faintly. 'Why didn't you tell me?'

'It's hardly relevant, is it?' she said, trying to disguise her intense discomfort beneath a cool façade. She tucked her legs underneath her and wrapped the ends of her cotton wrap over her knees.

'Bloody time-bomb!' He didn't bang his head against the striped silk wallpaper, but as he rested his brow against it he managed to give the impression he wanted to.

'I beg your pardon?'

He turned his head away from the wall and glared at her. 'You were twenty-two,' he exploded, his voice thick with resentment. 'I naturally assumed that should you become attracted to anyone you could be relied upon to act maturely. Do you honestly think I'd have suggested this arrangement if I'd known you hadn't explored your own sexuality? It's easy to see now why you're acting so irrationally—your hormones have finally caught up with you. You'll be hanging posters of boy bands on your wall next. I can see it all!' he taunted, closing his eyes on the awful mental image this conjured.

'My hormones or lack of them have got nothing to do with this. You don't trust me!'

'Trust you! I trust you about as much as I'd trust any adolescent experimenting with sex, and we all know how reliable they are.'

'I'm not experimenting with sex!' she burst out, her

face pink with a mixture of embarrassment and frustration. 'I really resent the implication I'm not a fit person to take care of Emma and Tom.'

'I know you care about Emma and Tom—that's not the problem we're facing here. You grew up too fast, Hannah. You didn't have the opportunity to be selfish.

'So now I'm selfish!'

'Tell me, what were you doing when other young people were being wild and irresponsible—experimenting with their freedom and lack of responsibilities? Shall I tell you?' He didn't give her the opportunity to reply. 'You were struggling to support yourself in some miserable bedsit somewhere. You were getting qualifications to earn a living and holding down part-time jobs to pay the bills. You missed out on a whole chunk of your youth. So why should I be surprised if you're trying to recapture it now?' The peculiar self-recrimination in his voice was more unsettling than his unreasonable accusations.

'How did you know...?' she began, amazed by the startling accuracy of the picture his soft words drew.

'You came into this house as an employee, remember. I followed up your references and it wasn't hard, knowing your background, to imagine what sort of life you'd had. A lot of the people I come across have had similar starts in life,' he reminded her. 'It's a road that all too frequently leads to the wrong side of the law. Not everyone is as single-minded and determined as you are.'

The immediate impression of quiet restraint and malleability had been the reason he'd missed the iron streak in her character. He suspected he was going to pay for this oversight—he already was paying!

'If you believe that, why do you doubt my ability to fulfil my obligation to the children?' His evaluation of her character came as something of a shock. Strangely, it made her feel less awkward about behaving naturally in front of him. 'I made a commitment and I won't do anything to compromise that.'

'You say that now, but what if you fall in love? Where would that leave our arrangement?'

'That's not possible,' she said hoarsely.

'A statement like that says everything about your inexperience,' he observed with the sort of lofty scorn that set her teeth on edge.

'What about you? You might fall in love.'

'I've been there and done that,' he said, his sexy mouth tightening with disapproval. 'The whole point I'm trying to make is you haven't.'

'Who says so?' she flung back recklessly.

'You mean you're not a...?'

'Just because you fall in love with someone, it doesn't necessarily follow that you sleep with them. I fell in love with someone who is unavailable.' Sometimes, she reflected, the truth—at least a cosmetic version of it, anyway—came in very handy!

'When did all this happen, or, rather, not happen?' he asked with insulting scepticism.

'Ages ago,' she said airily.

'Is he married?' he asked, frowning as he mentally reviewed all the married men who had shown any interest in his wife.

'I don't want to talk about it,' she replied with perfect honesty.

'Is it someone I know?'

'My private thoughts are one part of my life you can't control.'

'I don't try and control you!' he exclaimed in horrified denial.

'You're the one who cancelled my French classes,' she reminded him.

'We agreed—'

'*You* agreed,' she corrected him firmly. 'Like most of the decisions in this house, it was a strictly unilateral one.'

'I didn't think you minded,' he responded, his colour heightened. 'I had no intention of coercing you,' he added rather stiffly.

His austere glare had lost some of its power to intimidate her. It was partly her own fault, she acknowledged honestly. She'd never raised any objections to his habit of making all the decisions that affected her. It was fairly natural he'd assume she didn't have an opinion.

'Jean-Paul will be pleased to hear I'm not quitting.' Her steady stare openly challenged him.

An expression of reluctant admiration entered Ethan's eyes. 'The man seems to think you're his star pupil.'

'Who am I to argue?' It was about time she started standing up for herself. Winning certainly gave a girl a nice glow.

An expression of disgust crossed Ethan's face as he shook his head. 'I've never understood why women are such pushovers for pretty faces. 'He's so *obvious*,' he observed with distaste.

Hannah's mouth dropped open and her lip began to quiver. Had Ethan looked in the mirror recently? she wondered incredulously. He had more raw sex appeal in his little finger than dear Jean-Paul had in his entire body!

'What? What have I said now?'

When Ethan departed in disgust Hannah was curled on the bed in fits of helpless laughter.

*   *   *

It had been a week since the evening of their truce. A sort of normality reigned again. Hannah's more obvious scars had faded, with the exception of some multicoloured bruises across her ribcage and faint smudges on her arms. She'd been back to evening class, where there had been a noticeable absence of the dreaded Craig.

So she was in a loveless marriage—people survived worse situations. It was a matter of having a positive attitude. Her new attitude had been firmly in her mind today, when she'd cancelled the shopping trip with Alice. If she had to appear in her role as token wife when Ethan went to some friends' anniversary party, she was going to make the effort not to look like a fashion victim.

'The usual trim, madam?' her hairdresser had asked, disguising his boredom behind a professional smile.

'No, do something different.'

The carte blanche had been seized before she could retract her reckless invitation. Now, the sight of the growing heap of soft brown hair on the floor made Hannah feel a little queasy and she hardly dared look at her reflection. When she did she could hardly believe the transformation.

Cut just above shoulder-length, her cleverly layered mane framed her face in soft, feathery fingers. She could shake her head or rub her fingers through the silky ends and the cut sprang softly back into place.

'I look different.'

'I always knew you had potential.'

'I've got potential, she kept telling herself as she walked around town. The occasional glances she stole in the plate glass windows confirmed this pleasant theory. She'd never be beautiful, but potentially pretty might not be aiming too high.

She was walking in the direction of the expensive

store that Alice always took her to when a dress in a window display caught her eye. After a small internal struggle she decided to go in—the assistants couldn't be worse than the ones in the other store, who always gave her the most terrific inferiority complex with their snooty attitude and heavy make-up.

The middle-aged woman in the shop was neither snooty nor heavily made up. She did, however, shake her head slowly when Hannah mentioned the dress in the window. She ran a shrewd eye up and down Hannah's slim figure.

'Great frock, but you'd need at least another five inches to carry it off. Besides, the style is much too old for you. We do a really good petite range, though. Let's see what we've got.'

Without encouragement Hannah would never have tried the dress on. 'It's so…so red,' she said dubiously as she pirouetted in front of the mirror.

'It's sensational is what it is,' her one-woman fan club assured her. Hannah wondered cynically if she worked on commission. All the same, she thought, glancing into the full-length wall mirror, she hadn't known she was capable of looking—well, sexy!

The simple bodice of deep ruby-red satin was moulded closely but not tightly before it flared slightly into a short skirt. Sleeveless, with a scooped neck, it was the simplest thing she'd tried on. 'I usually wear sleeves—my arms are a bit skinny.'

'Are you mad? I'd kill for your arms, and your collarbones are so Audrey Hepburn,' the saleswoman sighed enviously. 'I expect you're too young to know who she is.'

Hannah grinned. 'I've seen *Breakfast at Tiffany's* a million times.'

I must have been mad, she thought later as she dithered at her bedroom door. What if Ethan hated it? What if he thought it looked, horror of horrors, *tarty*? What if he insisted she changed? What if…?

She shook her head angrily at these fancies. The fact was he probably wouldn't even notice she looked different. She was making a big fuss about nothing. What if he didn't like it—so what? *I* like it, she decided firmly.

This firm resolve carried her all the way to the drawing-room door. Getting beyond it was achieved by sheer will-power.

'Sorry if I'm late.' Her chin went automatically up to fend off any criticism. She was quite glad that the strappy sandals gave her an illusion of height.

Ethan was the sort of man whom nobody would ever mistake for a waiter in his dinner jacket. Whilst Hannah couldn't be described as a dispassionate observer, she couldn't believe anyone female could fail to be impressed by his sinfully sexy dark good looks.

He glanced from the file he was flicking through to his wristwatch. 'Only by five min…' He looked up and his voice froze as completely as his body. His eyes swept her from top to toe and back again before he spoke. 'You've cut your hair.'

'An impulse,' she said nervously. He'd noticed, but it was impossible to tell from his expression whether he approved of the transformation.

'Did Alice help you choose that?' His eyes touched the red dress.

'No.'

'It shows.'

Enigmatic could be pretty frustrating at times, she thought, glaring at his broad back as he moved in front of her to hold the door open.

Maggie Hilton and her husband, a couple ten years or so older than Ethan, were some of his closest friends. The very first dinner party she'd presided over as Mrs Kemp had been for them. Hannah had wanted everything to be perfect; she'd fussed and worried over the minutest detail for a whole week beforehand.

She'd been desperately anxious to do the right thing, say the right thing, but in the event she'd scarcely said anything. The couple were both solicitors and the conversation had been largely shop talk. Hannah would have liked to say something witty and amusing, but she didn't think they'd be interested in the funny thing that had happened outside the school gates. Occasionally someone would remember she was there and try to include her, but it had all been painfully forced.

She'd been settling Tom, who had woken whilst their guests were leaving. Richard had already got into the car, but Maggie had still been talking to Ethan in the hallway when she'd come quietly back downstairs.

'It's such a permanent solution, Ethan.'

'I know what I'm doing, Maggie.'

'Do you? I wonder? The children won't be small for ever, and then they'll be off to school. Oh, I know you had a horrid time at boarding-school, but you'll change your mind when the time comes, and, I don't care what anyone says, it builds character.'

Looking down from the dark alcove, Hannah could only see Ethan's back but Maggie's expression of pitying affection was highlighted by the light she stood beneath. 'She's very *nice*, but when I think of Catherine...' She shook her head regretfully. 'I know it wasn't all plain sailing, but the best of us have our differences— that's what makes marriage interesting. Catherine was

so alive and spontaneous, and she's so dull. I'm sorry—
I promised Richard I wouldn't say anything.'

'I think you should listen to your husband more often,
Maggie.'

'I know, but I've started now so I might as well be
hung for a sheep as a lamb! You have nothing in common. The poor girl has obviously never had anything to
do with people like us...'

'"People like us."' Ethan repeated the words slowly.
'I never had you pegged as a snob, Maggie.'

This accusation was hotly denied. 'I'm not sure you
did a kind thing, marrying her. She was obviously uncomfortable tonight—I felt quite sorry for her.'

'Your pity wasn't prominent when you brought
Catherine into the conversation at five-minute intervals.'

'Here with you it's only natural to think of Catherine;
you were a pair. She was your social and intellectual
equal, Ethan. I don't know how you can bring yourself
to—'

'Hannah may not have enjoyed our social and intellectual advantages, but she is bright. She's articulate and
thoughtful.'

Maggie Hilton conceded this with a sigh. 'I grant you
that, but she's so *dull*!'

'She's my wife.' It hadn't been a proud assertion, just
a flat statement of fact. He'd sounded like a man who'd
given up on hope.

Over time, when Hannah saw the Hiltons, she remembered that pitch of dull acceptance in his voice. But it
wouldn't be so bad tonight: she'd gained confidence
over the last year, and had learnt a few social tricks. She
was still an outsider as far as they were concerned, and
she accepted the fact.

Ethan didn't say another word to her until they stood

outside the illuminated façade of the Hiltons' home, and even then she had to prompt him.

'Didn't I get it all off?' she asked when his eyes dwelt over-long in the general direction of her mouth. She touched her lips nervously. 'The red lipstick was too much,' she babbled frantically, 'but I thought I'd got it all off.' It had left a crimson stain that made her look as if she'd been eating raspberries, but she thought she'd removed the worst of the 'in your face' gloss.

'Let me see,' Ethan said, placing his forefinger firmly under her chin. 'There's only one sure way to remove lipstick in my experience.'

'What's…?'

The sensuous, slow movement of his warm mouth against her lips sent any lingering concerns about her make-up out of the window. She wasn't the slightest bit bothered when his big hands slid through the silky strands of her hair, obliterating her new hairstyle as his fingers caressed her scalp. The tingling went all the way down to her toes and she was obliged to press her hands against the solidity of his chest to stop herself falling into an inelegant heap.

'Mission accomplished,' he murmured, drawing away. His eyes appeared darker than usual as he examined her quivering lips.

Hannah was dizzily aware that the door was opening. 'Thank you,' she said faintly.

'It was a pleasure.'

'It was?' she asked doubtfully. She pinned her polite social smile on her face as her hostess appeared.

'Definitely.' He flicked a look in her direction which made her stomach dissolve into a warm ache before he surged forward to hug the elegant older woman. 'Maggie, my dear, you look marvellous.'

'Thank you, Ethan, darling, but I know when I've been upstaged,' she said drily, staring at Hannah, who stood a little behind them. 'Poor Richard, I'm afraid his blood pressure is going to be troublesome tonight. You look stunning, my dear.' For a moment Hannah assumed it was Ethan her hostess was talking to; when her error became obvious her eyes widened.

Ethan caught Hannah's hand and urged her gently into the brilliantly lit hallway. 'Doesn't she just?'

Did he actually believe that or was this a sample of his silky society manners? When he chose to wheel out the charm Ethan could leave even Jean-Paul standing, only he didn't normally waste his charisma on his wife. It would be a mistake to read too much into this behaviour, she told herself firmly, and as for the kiss. The kiss…! She couldn't think at all when she thought about that.

She couldn't help but be gratified by the double takes and flattering attention. Alice was very condescending in her helpful criticism of Hannah's outfit, and Hannah couldn't resist pointing out that the lady's own husband had admired her outfit.

'But he's a man, my dear, and men are notoriously drawn to…tacky— Sorry.' She laughed theatrically and covered her mouth with a hand. 'It just slipped out. Don't look so unhappy, Hannah. Its not as if you've got a lot to flaunt, is it?'

'Not as much as you,' Hannah agreed quietly as she turned to go. She regretted immediately that she'd allowed herself to be goaded into the catty response. 'I wish I hadn't said that,' she murmured, closing her eyes.

'If she can't take it, the lady shouldn't dish it up.'

The sound of Ethan's voice at her elbow made Hannah jump. 'Were you eavesdropping?'

'Not intentionally. You've danced with everyone else,' he said, as the soft heavy thud of an evocative melody filled the room. 'I think it's my turn.' He took hold of her upper arm, and his fingers slid experimentally over her skin as if he was somehow impelled to sample the texture of her creamy flesh.

'I didn't think you danced.' The almost imperceptible movement of his fingers had a mesmeric effect on Hannah's nervous system. Why had he kissed her? It was a question that wouldn't go away. Each time her thoughts had returned to the subject her eyes had sought him out. The light food and wine hadn't taken the taste of him from her mouth. Her throat ached with emotion. And no practical good intentions could banish the excitement that heated her blood.

'It was news to me that you do,' he reminded her drily. 'If dancing is what they call those sexy gyrations you've been treating us to tonight.'

Sexy, me? Not for the first time that evening her eyes collided with his, but this time she didn't have the comfort of a room's distance between them. 'I've never learnt to dance properly,' she babbled in panic as his arm went around her waist.

'Then we'll leave the dips and twirls to the people who know what they're doing, shall we?' He took one of her hands and placed it against his shoulder. 'Shuffle step will do just fine. You can't deny you don't have an ear for rhythm after tonight.'

'I can't?' She couldn't attribute the light-headed sensation to the glass of wine she'd nursed throughout the evening. Her proximity to Ethan was a much more powerful drug.

Her legs were pressed against his hard thighs as they moved around the impromptu dance floor. Without doing anything obvious Ethan had unobtrusively drawn her closer. To prevent her hand being squashed between their bodies she had sensibly placed it out of harm's way around his neck. Her fingertips lightly trailed across the area where his dark, thick hair ended in crisp curls.

As the music throbbed Ethan dropped his head until she could feel the warmth of his breath stirring the glossy strands of hair on her head. 'What do you smell of? I don't recognise the perfume.'

'Shampoo, probably. I don't possess any expensive perfumes.' She almost stumbled when his hand slid down from her waist and his fingers splayed over the rounded contour of her behind. 'These heels,' she laughed, recovering her balance but not her equilibrium. Was he doing this on purpose, and, if so, to what end? The heat of his body was absorbed by the thin fabric of her dress and passed directly into her own skin.

'You've got good legs.' Somehow he managed to in- sinuate one of her legs between his. She grunted softly in shock as she felt the evidence of his arousal graze the crest of her hip before a slight twist of his body moved the pressure to her lower belly.

'If they were six inches longer.' Catherine had been tall, very tall, a Nordic-looking beauty. Hannah wished she hadn't spoilt the moment by thinking of her.

'There's nothing wrong with being petite—small but perfectly formed.'

'If I agreed with you I'd sound conceited,' she said, trying to sound as if his words hadn't raised her excite- ment levels to a new high. 'If I denied it I'd sound coy.' The effort to be cool took its toll, and she surrendered to the invitation of his broad chest with a small sigh. 'I'm a bit tired,' she murmured in a husky voice, just in case he got the wrong, or rather *right* idea.

'Let's go home.'

'Now?' she faltered, lifting her head as the slow beat was replaced by a livelier tune. 'It's early.'

'I'm sure it's difficult to tear yourself away, but I'm less keen on the spectacle of grown men drooling over my wife.'

'Are you suggesting I was encouraging them?' Her hands slid down his dark-suited forearms and with a small flick of his wrists his fingers closed around hers.

'The transformation from wallflower to belle of the ball must be a pretty intoxicating one—I wouldn't blame you if you enjoyed flirting. I was afraid this would happen,' he mused, watching her broodingly.

'I don't know what you're talking about.'

He looked into the puzzled depths of her clear eyes. 'I know,' he said heavily. 'Come on, we'll make our apologies and leave.'

Richard Hilton insisted on seeing them out himself. He placed an arm around Hannah's shoulders and she could smell the alcohol on his breath. She didn't much mind—he made an amiable, if garrulous drunk.

'I keep telling her she looks gorgeous,' he announced, slapping Ethan heartily on the back. 'You sly dog, you knew what you were about. Like I said to Maggie, nobody knows what goes on behind closed doors.' He tapped the side of his nose and gave a conspiratorial wink. 'I never said you were a fool.'

'I'm touched,' Ethan said, detaching himself gently but firmly from a maudlin embrace. 'We must go.'

'Yes, that's it, off you go. Would myself in your place.'

Hannah laughed as they walked over to the car. She was determined to show him she wasn't reading anything into his friend's drunken and deeply embarrassing ramblings. 'Richard seems to think we're leaving early to—'

'Do unspeakable things behind closed doors,' Ethan finished smoothly. 'A crazy idea.'

'He's had a lot to drink.' It was hard to sound suitably amused when she had the distinct impression that under the superficially bland expression Ethan wasn't laughing at all; he wasn't even smiling.

'Don't let that bumbling air fool you—I've seen Richard win at poker after imbibing enough to sink a battle cruiser. A very perceptive man,' he mused half to himself. In the darkness she could see the silver flash of his disturbing eyes.

It would be a mistake, she decided, to read anything at all into this cryptic utterance—but of course she did.

CHAPTER FOUR

WHEN the car drew to a halt outside The Manor House Hannah didn't move. She had to know.

'Why did you kiss me, Ethan?'

He clicked open his seat belt and turned slowly in his seat. From what she could make out in the semi-darkness he was less surprised by her question than she was.

'I thought I'd get in first.'

'First?'

'Before someone else did. You look very kissable tonight, Hannah.'

She caught her breath at this husky admission. 'I didn't kiss anyone else tonight.' And she hadn't wanted to, she thought, clasping her hands tightly in her lap to stop herself reaching out for him.

'Only because I brought you home before the wolves closed in.' His jaw tightened as he recalled the increasing rage that had built up inside him as he'd watched men ogling his wife. The last man to say something complimentary about her to him had received a murderous glare and retreated looking shaken. Ethan had felt slightly ashamed. In the darkness he paused soberly to examine the violence of his revulsion.

This fanciful description of his very respectable friends brought a gurgle of laughter to Hannah's lips. She felt the silent disapproval of his response to her amusement in the darkness.

'Isn't that a tad dramatic?' she asked.

'You really are determined to make up for lost time,

aren't you?' She could hear him grating his teeth. 'Don't you realise what you could destroy if you insist on experimenting?'

'I only cut my hair and bought a new dress,' she protested. 'It's not my fault if people are so influenced by superficial things.' And he was as bad as any of them, she thought resentfully. Kissing her, dancing with her...inviting her lurid imagination to go into overdrive.

'The change goes a lot deeper than that, Hannah.'

'Well, I'm sorry if you don't like it, Ethan, but I'm a lot happier being myself. Don't worry, I'm not going to jump into bed with the first man who tells me I'm beautiful. That would be taking gratitude to extremes.' It was insulting that he imagined she'd be such a push-over.

'What if that man is your husband?' It wasn't a sudden notion—it just came out that way. He'd been turning the idea over in his head all week. Tonight just made the need for action more urgent.

'What?' she whispered, unable to believe he'd actually said what she thought.

'If you need to discover your sexuality it would be safer for all concerned if you did so with me,' he observed casually. The darkness concealed the fact he was looking far from casual as he tensely awaited her reply.

'I'm touched by your willingness to make such a sacrifice,' she said, her voice shaking. 'Thanks, but no, thanks, Ethan! I'm not that desperate. What's wrong? Didn't you believe me when I said I wouldn't try for an annulment? Did the ultimate sacrifice seem the best way to close off that avenue of escape?' Now she thought about it, it all made awful sense.

She struggled with the handle of the passenger door. Her free hand flailed wildly back at him as he tried to prevent her getting out. As Ethan reached out to stop her escaping his hand came into contact with the spot where her lace-topped stocking ended and her bare thigh began. It had seemed for a split second that his fingers had begun to move experimentally, but he drew back so abruptly she knew she must have been mistaken.

'You imagine I'd be that cold-blooded?' His voice sounded strange and forced in the enclosed space of the car.

'I think you can be ruthlessly practical when it suits you. The facts do speak for themselves. You never looked twice at me before I suggested a divorce.' To her intense relief the door finally opened and she half fell out of the car. Happily this one was stationary.

'You can't think of any other reason why I want you in my bed?' he yelled after her.

Just as well their nearest neighbour was a field away. She could hear his long legs catching up with her shorter stride as she reached the front door. The housekeeper always stayed overnight on the occasions she babysat and she would be long since in bed. Short of waking the entire household, Hannah didn't have much choice but to wait for Ethan.

'I don't have a key.' Her back was pressed against the door as she faced him.

Ethan was breathing hard; his face was shadowed, but she could see he was angry—really angry. She'd never seen him so close to losing control before. A small, objective portion of her mind was amazed that she'd been responsible for this. The rest of her brain wasn't objective—it was a mess of scattered half-formed thoughts.

Her intense visceral reaction to his suggestion wouldn't have been so intense if she hadn't been so hopelessly in love with him. The pragmatic proposal

seemed a cruel parody of what she'd longed for and it
had cut painfully deep.

He pressed one hand against the wall beside her head
as he silently unlocked the door. In the shadow of his
body she felt as if she were cocooned in a cave, only
the walls weren't cold stone, they were warm, living
flesh. As the door swung open she ducked under his arm.

'Not so fast.' He stepped after her and caught her by
the shoulder, sending her swirling round a hundred and
eighty degrees. The fact that she'd have fallen off her
heels didn't really matter, because he literally swept her
off her feet as he jerked her towards him.

He wasn't satisfied with a submissive response; he
wanted surrender—and he got it. He didn't stop until
he'd felt the small, guttural moans of pleasure in her
throat, parried the darting forays of her tongue with his
own and reduced her body to a trembling, boneless mass
of screaming nerve-endings.

Gasping for breath, he pulled away, and Hannah was
horrified to see her fingers still twisted in his hair.
Shaking, she pulled her nerveless hands free. Taking her
by her shoulders, he looked so savage that for a minute
she thought he was going to shake her.

'That cold-blooded enough for you?'

Cold-blooded! It had been ruthless—a fact that appeared to be slowly dawning on Ethan too. A spasm of
something that might have been regret crossed his features.

'It was most impressive, darling,' a strange voice
commented. 'Would you like a cup of tea? Drew has
just made a pot.'

'Mother!' Incredulously Ethan focused on the figure
casually seated at the head of the long table. 'What are
you doing here? And who the hell's Drew?' He looked

without enthusiasm at the tall blond young man who was calmly pouring milk into a mug.

'Didn't I say he'd be delighted to see me? It brings tears to my eyes every time I remember him saying to me, "This will always be your home, Mother." So touching.' She dabbed at invisible spots of moisture at the corners of her eyes. 'Drew is a *dear* friend of mine who has travelled all the way from Patagonia with me.' Since she'd been widowed, Faith Kemp had indulged her passion for foreign travel, and usually the odd card from exotic places was the only reminder of her existence.

'Geography never was my best subject, Mother.'

If being caught passionately kissing his wife had embarrassed him, he was hiding it well. Hannah, on the other hand, was wishing she were invisible. Wishing didn't help—she was the focus of her mother-in-law's ill-concealed interest and the silent stranger's blue-eyed sympathy as his sharp gaze noted the faded bruises along her shoulder.

'South America, darling. Some people actually speak Welsh there—extraordinary! My great-grandmother was Welsh; did I ever mention it?'

'Yes.' From his expression it was plain that Ethan was less than fascinated by the lesson.

'Andrew Cummings.' The tall man moved forward, his hand extended. He wore faded jeans and a tee shirt, and a tatty army surplus jacket was hung on the back of a chair. His sun-bleached blond hair was almost long enough to tie back in a ponytail, which would have been in keeping with his unconventional image. For an awful moment Hannah thought Ethan was going to ignore the hand. 'I can see I'm intruding.' Drew's voice was low and cultured—an educated bohemian, Hannah decided.

Hannah rushed in before Ethan could agree. 'Nonsense—there's plenty of room here. Isn't there, Ethan?' she insisted, glaring at him.

'Of course,' Ethan responded. His reluctance was obvious enough to make Hannah blush. She was beginning to feel quite sorry for the stranger.

'I'll show you to a room,' she put in quickly, seizing the opportunity to escape. She thought for a moment that Ethan was going to object, and breathed a sigh of relief when he nodded.

She'd mounted the stairs, their unexpected guest bringing up the rear, when Ethan's deep voice seemed to vibrate off the vaulted ceiling.

'Well, if you think you're sharing a room with your toy boy under my roof, Mother, you're mistaken.'

'My God,' his parent replied clearly, 'you always were an awful prude! I'm curious, Ethan—how exactly are you planning to stop me? Are you planning on patrolling the house all night?'

Hannah risked a look at the blond young man's profile; much to her relief and amazement, he looked amused.

'Sorry.'

'Don't worry about it, I've been called a lot worse.' He unslung his backpack as Hannah paused outside a bedroom door. 'It's me who should be apologising—I had assumed Faith had warned you we were coming. But then she's rather fond of the element of surprise,' he mused with a reminiscent smile.

'I wouldn't know. I haven't seen her since our wedding day.' To her horror Hannah realised that she was close to tears. 'If you want anything, just yell,' she said hurriedly as she opened the door and stepped to one side for him to enter.

'I think I should be saying that,' Drew observed bluntly. He'd have to be made of stone not to pick up the distress this girl was emanating. That, along with her surly husband's attitude and the traces of old bruises, told a story that filled him with anger. The man was obviously a thug.

Hannah flushed as the implication of his words sank in. 'I think you've misread the situation,' she said stiffly.

'It happens,' he agreed with an easy shrug. 'But the offer stands,' he said firmly.

Going back to her room, Hannah reflected ruefully that it was lucky Ethan hadn't heard the conversation. She could imagine he just might take exception to the idea that his wife needed protecting—especially if it was him she needed protecting from!

She'd knocked the bedside light over trying to switch it on. The lamp lay on the floor, its shade at a crazy angle, casting shadows over the deep blue carpet.

Her cream cotton nightshirt was wet with perspiration and she was shaking. It wasn't the first time she'd had the nightmare of being trapped in the car with Craig, but it was the worst.

Her breathing was just calming when the door burst open and their blond-haired guest appeared. His blue eyes swept the room suspiciously before he moved inside.

'What are you doing?' she asked, surprisingly unalarmed by the intrusion.

'You yelled.'

'Sorry about that. I had a nightmare.'

'So I see.' He bent to pick up the lamp from the floor.

'Why the hell did you lock the door, Hannah?' Ethan's eyes narrowed into slits when he saw the well-built and scantily dressed figure of Drew Cummings. 'I'm sure there's a perfectly logical explanation for the fact you're in my wife's bedroom at one a.m.' The soft hostility in his voice was more threatening than any raised voice might have been. 'I suggest you share it— now!'

Broad-shouldered and lean-hipped, Ethan was wearing light silk shorts which did nothing to disguise the athletic power of his tall frame. Hannah felt forbidden stirrings just looking at him. Feelings that had been quite absent when she'd looked at Drew, even though they were similarly attired. Sexual chemistry certainly didn't follow any logical pattern.

To give him his due, Drew didn't recoil from the dark suspicion in Ethan's voice. The edgy atmosphere was heavy with the threat of imminent violence.

'She yelled out. I'm a light sleeper.'

Hannah knew she hadn't imagined the warning held in this statement.

'Are you all right, Hannah?' Ethan's hard glance flicked in her direction.

'Just a nightmare. Thank you, Drew, but I'm fine now.' Please let him go before things get really silly! Considering the fact that until recently the only male who had ventured across her threshold had been a three-year-old child, it occurred to her that she was taking two virile, extremely attractive men circling each other with wary aggression quite calmly.

Drew's blue eyes rested on Ethan with a less than friendly expression. 'If *you* say so.'

'I do.' She gave a sigh of relief as he departed. She whistled softly and sank back against the pillows.

'What was all that about?' Ethan asked, closing the door firmly behind him.

'He appears to think I need protecting.'

'From what?'

'You, I imagine,' she confessed as a bubble of inappropriate laughter rose up in her throat.

'And how did he get that impression?'

'Don't look at me, I didn't say a word. It might have something to do with first impressions,' she mused, throwing him a wry look.

'I don't like being looked at as if I'm a wife-beater,' he growled, in an outraged tone.

'Any more than I like being looked at like a victim. Shall we stop the conversation right there while we're in unexpected harmony?' Her eyes widened in alarm as he sat on the edge of the bed. The light thrown out by the small lamp shadowed the strong curves of his back, highlighting the shift of muscles as he moved. His skin looked so smooth, almost oiled; she wondered what it would be like to rub oil into the hard contours.

'I don't like him.'

'I'd never have guessed.'

'What do you suppose would have happened if I hadn't walked in when I did?'

'You obviously have a theory—do share it,' she urged, propping her chin on her hands. 'I'm all ears.'

'I doubt if it's your ears he's interested in. Prowling around half naked,' he said sourly.

'Like you.' This provocative little jibe earned her a savage glare. She widened her eyes with an innocent confusion that made him grind his teeth audibly. The confusion wasn't entirely faked: she'd let her eyes dwell on the firm contours of his lean, tanned body for longer than was good for her.

'This is *my* house.'

'This is *my* bedroom.'

'You're very territorial all of a sudden.'

'I'm very popular all of a sudden,' she countered drily. It was difficult to be flattered when she knew from experience to what lengths Ethan was willing to go to safeguard his children's happiness.

'I find it bloody perverse that you're willing to give a total stranger the benefit of the doubt, but you attach the basest motives possible to everything I do.'

'You don't have to seduce me, Ethan. I'm not about to run off with Drew or anyone else, even if he is charming and *very* good-looking.'

'My mother certainly thinks so.'

'I don't think your mother is the sort of person who takes kindly to being told how to run her life, especially by her son,' Hannah ventured warily. 'At least, that was the impression I got,' she observed with a shrug. Like her son, Faith didn't seem the type to take advice kindly.

'Forget about my mother,' he said. The thickness in his voice filled her with alarm and excitement. 'Why must I have some ulterior motive in wanting to seduce my wife? Your words not mine,' he added wryly. 'Why can't I just be responding to a basic biological need— the most basic biological need there is?'

'If your biological needs had been a priority in your choice of wife you wouldn't have married me, Ethan.' The honest truth hurt, but she didn't want him to believe she was under any illusions, though sometimes she wished she were! She had to prove to herself as well as to him that she couldn't be beguiled by the smouldering expression in his eyes. 'You're not sexually attracted to me,' she said firmly.

'Is that a fact?'

'I know I'm not beautiful.'

'If men only slept with beautiful women we'd have a serious under-population problem.'

'You mean you're prepared to close your eyes and think of Cindy Crawford! I'm seriously disappointed in you, Ethan. I thought you were much slicker than that!' Her small bosom rose swiftly in outrage.

'Oh, hell, that came out all wrong!' She wasn't even sure he was aware that his hand was massaging the length of her thigh over the down-filled guilt. She wished she weren't so profoundly aware; even through the layers, the contact sent electrical thrills shooting through her body. 'I meant that beauty is a subjective thing. I can admire a beautiful woman without wanting to make love to her.'

Hannah didn't bother to hide her scepticism. This claim didn't tally with the popular conception of the male animal, and, lacking any personal experience to speak about, that was all she had to go on.

'If you think you're unattractive people will treat you that way,' he said in a persuasively positive tone. 'It's all a matter of the aura you project. Tonight you felt sexy and people found you sexy.'

'I...'

'Don't deny it. It was obvious and justified—you did look sexy.'

'A dress and the right accessories are all superficial. Next you'll be telling me I'm beautiful inside.' She tried to sound flippant but it was difficult. Her voice emerged painfully husky. As he developed his theme she found herself wanting more and more to believe all the flattering things he was saying.

'Maybe you are. Kids and animals love you, and they're supposed to know about these things, although personally I've always found them undiscriminating little beasts.' Hannah wasn't sure if he was talking about children or animals. 'As far as I'm concerned,' he continued, fixing her with a very direct stare, 'you've turned into a right royal pain in the proverbial.'

She gasped indignantly at this cool observation. 'Well, *thank you*! I've turned myself inside out trying to make life comfortable for you, and the first time something goes a bit wrong you act like a sulky prima donna! I think you're the most unreasonable, selfish man I've ever met! All take and no give.'

'I'm not big on self-analysis, but just lately I've come to the conclusion I've got a deep-seated masochistic streak,' he confided. 'Apart from the odd steamy dream about that adjoining door. There's something about a closed door,' he mused moodily, 'that invites speculation.'

Hannah choked at this throw-away remark, unable to believe her ears. She felt a tell-tale heat burn her cheeks. Was it possible that he'd been having fantasies that side of the door whilst she…? Had their fantasies had much in common? she wondered.

'I took your contribution to this house pretty much for granted,' Ethan continued, noting her expression with a look of satisfaction. 'The moment you start developing attitude, all I can think about is ripping off your clothes,' he said frankly.

'Attitude?' she said faintly.

'Gallons of the stuff,' he reaffirmed grimly. 'I also happen to like your face. You remind me of one of those Madonna paintings—it's possible the medieval females who posed for those were real pains too.'

'Perhaps you think sex is as good a way as any of keeping me in line. Perhaps you're a control freak!' she accused wildly. He was pushing all the right buttons;

she had to do something! Or any minute now she'd be...
She closed her eyes, unwilling to contemplate what she
might be doing next.

His eyebrows shot up to his hairline and he regarded
her with a virtuous expression. 'It must have something
to do with my careless use of the term "masochism",
but I think you've got entirely the wrong idea about the
sort of sex I have in mind, Hannah. I'm not into *that*
sort of thing,' he admitted apologetically.

A gurgling sound escaped the confines of her throat.
'I didn't mean...I...' She swallowed to clear the con-
gestion of scorching embarrassment. 'Oh, you're impossible!'

'Up to this point, nothing short of thumbscrews could
have prised an honest opinion out of you. Now you're
flinging insults. I call that progress.'

'You're weird.' She glared at him with baffled exas-
peration.

'Insults are intimate,' he explained.

The way his velvet tongue caressed 'intimate' made
the fine hairs on her nape stand on end. 'I thought they
were indicative of incompatibility.' The frost that was
supposed to coat her words thawed the moment she
opened her mouth.

'We've never tried to see if we're compatible.'

'That's the way you wanted it.'

'And you didn't? Come off it, Hannah, you've spent
the last year pretending I wasn't actually here. It was
obvious I was the only part of this deal you found hard
to stomach, and I didn't mind.' Much, he added silently.
There had been times when he'd felt slightly irked that
she showed no interest whatever in the things he did.
But he'd accepted he was nothing but a pay packet to
her. 'The less time I spent here, the more you liked it!'

She wasn't about to say anything that might give a slightly more accurate slant to his interpretation of the past year. 'So what's changed?'

'We both have, I think.'

'No!' She shook her head, refusing to take the next step. He was confusing her with clever words. She couldn't trust him; she couldn't trust herself!

'My mother says she's getting married.' He dropped the bombshell at the most unexpected moment.'

'Not Drew!' she gasped, forgetting for a moment he'd manoeuvred her into a corner. 'Oh, Ethan, you didn't read her a lecture, did you?' she asked anxiously. She knew how tactless he could be when he got protective.

'See what I mean—you've lost your touch with the old cold indifference. You care, and not just about the children,' he said triumphantly.

'You rat!' she cried. 'I hope you're not trying to imply I'm in love with you.' She had been scorching hot seconds before; now shock left her trembling with cold.

'Of course I'm not.'

She could have throttled him when he had the insensitive gall to laugh. 'I suppose you made that up—about your mother?

'I wish I had. No, it looks like Galahad—with a scornful expression, he jerked his head toward the door '—is the lucky man. Whilst she didn't name him, that was the impression I got.'

'Drew? He can't be any older than you.' Faith Kemp was a good-looking woman, but there was no disguising the fact that she was of a different generation from that of her companion. Hannah couldn't help feeling shocked, even though she knew conditioning had a lot to do with her gut response.

'A year younger,' he observed gloomily. 'Thirty-

five—she told me so herself. I can't believe that she'd
be stupid enough to fall for some itinerant beach bum.'

'He seemed very nice,' Hannah felt impelled to pro-
test. 'You don't know he's a beach bum.'

'I know his type,' Ethan observed with a sneer.

'Nonsense!' she contradicted firmly, and earned herself a scowl. 'And I don't suppose you'd be shocked if
it was your *father* marrying a girl twenty—'

'Thirty years younger, and I'd be very shocked, considering he's been six feet under for the past ten years!
Anyway,' he said with a frown, 'you're very eager to
defend mum's toy boy all of a sudden. Perhaps that's
why the door was locked? You didn't want me to inter-
rupt.'

'Sure, I propositioned Drew on the way up the stairs.
I'm quite a girl!' she drawled sarcastically.

'The man's a gigolo; he doesn't need an invitation.'

'For goodness' sake, Ethan, anyone would think
you're jealous.'

'Wouldn't any man who found that opportunist little
creep in his wife's bedroom half naked—' he swallowed
hard, having difficulty containing his contempt '—have
just cause to be suspicious?'

'But I'm not really your wife.'

'That can soon be fixed.' His eyes flicked to her
shocked face. 'I think we'd both like that.' He reached
out and touched her cheek; his fingers left a trail of fire
against her skin. 'You look as if I've made an improper
suggestion. We're married—nothing could be more
proper than for us to share a bed.' The lazy amusement
was superficial; there was nothing lazy about the expression on his watchful face or the tension in his
big body.

'It's a big house—there are plenty of beds.' Inside her breast her heart was beating a wild tattoo.

'Lonely beds. Aren't you lonely in this big bed, Hannah? Why look for someone else to fill it when I'm so handy?'

Looking at him, hearing the soft, inviting purr of his voice, brought a wildlife documentary on predators she'd seen recently irresistibly to mind. So he didn't have sharp claws and a silky pelt—he definitely filled all the other criteria for predator, and she identified totally with the helpless situation of the creature being stalked.

'Sometimes—sometimes I'm lonely,' she admitted breathily. 'But I'm used to it.' The impulse to turn her cheek into the palm of his hand proved too strong to resist. Rubbing her cheek against the slightly callused surface of his hand, she closed her eyes. What's wrong with me? she wondered. A plea of convenience was hardly the most wildly romantic form of seduction, and yet here she was literally panting for his touch.

She recognised that she was fast approaching the point where she wouldn't care what his motivations were. The prospect of reaching a point of mindless acceptance was not entirely an unpleasant one—it was definitely a hotly exciting one.

'This wasn't part of the deal.' She had to put up some sort of defence. It was scary to realise how much she hoped he'd dispose of her last feeble objections with his usual efficiency.

'It wasn't something we excluded. Circumstances change, situations alter... If you're going to fall in love, it might as well be with me.'

'I don't want to fall in love.' He couldn't know the irony of his words, or how much the humorous twist of

his lips hurt. 'Has anyone ever told you you're a manip-
ulative bastard?' she asked hoarsely.

'Do you realise that you'd never have said that to me
a couple of weeks ago?' He didn't seem to be put out
by her forcibly expressed condemnation.

'Probably not, but I might have thought it!'

'I bet you did. Why do you think you're doing it
now?'

'Because we...you...we didn't talk then.'

'Or fight, or argue, or kiss,' he added triumphantly.

Meaning that something had altered. Was that something him or her?

'You knew exactly how attracted to you I was when
we danced tonight. It wasn't something I could disguise.'
He bent closer so the last words were murmured into
her ear. 'You were excited,' he told her throatily. He
took her face firmly between his hands. 'You liked it.'

'Yes, yes...' she admitted, her eyes glistening with
emotional tears as she met the challenge of his stare. His
face was so close she could see the fine lines that radi-
ated from the corners of his eyes, see the gold tips on
the end of his dark eyelashes, and see the faint silvery
line of a scar just below his left eye.

'Our marriage has worked, hasn't it?' His thumb ran
softly over the quivering outline of her slightly parted
lips. 'Why shouldn't this?' He encountered no opposi-
tion when he gently pressed against her breastbone and
sent her back against the soft pillows. Supported on his
elbow, his long body settled beside her. 'Your hormones
are raging, and don't bother denying it. I recognise the
symptoms—probably because mine are rioting too,' he
added drily.

Ethan with riotous hormones! The idea held a unique
fascination for her. 'It makes things complicated.' The
idea of placing her hand against the flat-ridged muscles

of his belly took root in her mind and swiftly became an obsessive thought.

'We're not losing anything, Hannah,' he soothed her huskily. 'If anything, we're gaining something new— something that will strengthen what we have. Complicated is when we start looking outside this house for fulfilment. And you will,' he said, reading the denial in her eyes.

The convenience factor reared its ugly head again, and it roused her sufficiently to fight against the inevitable. 'You make it sound as if I've no more choice than an animal on heat,' she protested, distressed by the mental parallel she drew.

'We all try and deny it, but primitive instincts are never very far from the surface, no matter how sophisticated we like to think ourselves. Don't underestimate a primal need.'

The rasp of his voice made her shudder. 'I can't imagine you losing control.' The idea sent ripples of delicious excitement through her body. 'You're so disciplined.'

If she leaned forward and pressed her lips against his hair-roughened chest, would that be enough to make him lose control? Or would it take more...' Eyes half closed, she caught her full lower lip between her even white teeth and looked with hungry curiosity at his face. The fantasy in her head intensified until nothing else existed.

'If you carry on looking at me like that you'll soon learn different,' he growled, his chest rising as he exhaled deeply. 'You do want this to happen, don't you?'

'Yes, yes...yes!' Her voice grew muffled as her face burrowed into his chest. An expression of fierce satisfaction flared on his taut face before his arms came automatically around her.

'That's as good a place to start as any.' A strong shud-

der ran through his body as the tip of her tongue touched
the warm skin of his chest.

Feeling his shocked recoil, she stopped. 'Sorry,' she
said, immediately raising her head. 'I'd been thinking
about it and it just sort of...' She gazed at him guiltily.
Her ignorance of the unwritten rules of sexual etiquette
was rather frustrating.

Ethan didn't look too offended. In fact, beneath the
heat of desire his eyes were filled with warmth and
amusement. 'Perhaps we should start with the things
you've been thinking about.' His sinfully sexy drawl fed
the flames that were making her dizzy with desire.

'I just wondered what you tasted like.'

'And?'

The corners of her mouth lifted as she recalled the
salty tang of his skin. 'Nice.'

'I like the taste part too.' Her mind was immediately
invaded by a series of steamy, hair-curling pictures to
match his provocative words. 'Only I think it might be
an idea to start with the kissing stage and progress...'

Kissing was all right—kissing was good, and at least
she wasn't a total novice in the kissing stakes. 'I'm in
your hands.'

Her wicked little smile knocked him for six yet again.
He kissed the smile off her lips. He drove every thought
and preconceived idea out of her head with a bewilder-
ing alternation between greedy, driving hunger and play-
ful, soft torment.

'Oh, I love your mouth,' she breathed fervently, when
she was able to breathe once more. She tensed slightly
as she realised his fingers were skilfully slipping the
loops that held the bodice of her nightshirt together.

His mouth nuzzled the slender column of her neck

before he reached eye-level. 'What's wrong?'

'I'm not very—I'm too thin.'

'Who said so?' he asked with tolerant amusement.

'You,' she reminded him bluntly.

'What a time to start taking any notice of what I say. I want to see your body. I want to feel it against me. I want to taste it. I want to see if that blush of yours goes all over. I've given the subject a lot of thought just lately.'

'You have?'

He nodded firmly. 'Take it off for me,' he instructed huskily, unable to resist the opportunity to fulfil part of a recurrent dream he'd had—a dream that went back further than the last week.

On her knees now, Hannah pulled the nightshirt over her head and let it slip silently to the floor. Half of her wanted to look away, but the other half knew she'd see his real reaction in that split second. She was right—in that split second his face was naked and strangely defenceless. The intensity of the passion in his eyes had an odd, unfocused blindness. Under her amazed eyes she saw him fight and overcome the strong passions that drove him.

She could now believe and wonder at his hoarse, 'My God, you're so lovely.' And when he said, 'Come here,' she did so willingly. Physically the distance was small, but emotionally it was a leap of faith.

His back was propped up against the bed-head, and she was kneeling, straddling him. His hands glided smoothly over the graceful line of her spine, curving possessively over the firm contours of her bottom. Raising his knee slightly, he touched the sensitive, aching apex between her legs and drew a low moan from her dry throat.

His eyes never strayed from her flushed, aroused face as he changed the angle of the raised leg and sent her sliding downwards until the damp, tangled patch between her thighs was forced against his hip and her breasts were flattened against his chest. The silk boxers he wore were darkened where the dampness of his skin made them cling to his body, and they could barely contain the evidence of his growing desire.

Whilst his lips tugged and sucked at hers, his capable hands slid under her knees, and suddenly she was sitting astride him with her flexed legs pressed up and along either side of his body. He ran his hands down the back of her thighs and used the space between them to manoeuvre himself close enough to claim the twin pleasures of her aching breasts.

All thoughts of inadequacy vanished from her head as he teased the ruched peaks. She felt womanly and irresistible as his teeth and tongue made her breasts tingle and burn.

'When you touch me here,' she said shyly, bringing one finger up to indicate one erect nipple, 'I can feel it here.' She moved her hand to indicate her lower belly, where the muscle spasms clenched her womb in a series of deeply pleasurable contortions. Was this what it was like to be a woman? she wondered with awe. 'I wish I'd known,' she said, turning her sleepily sexy stare on him.

Her actions seemed to stir *him* to action—surging, violent action. Suddenly she was flat on her back and he was over her. She could see the gleam of sweat glistening on the muscle-packed contours of his shoulders and chest.

With one finger he drew a line from the pulse spot in the hollow at the base of her throat, between the valley of her breasts, over her flat belly.

'Here?' he asked hoarsely. 'And here?' He slipped his fingers between her legs and sucked in air noisily as she gasped, her body bucking. The slick heat that greeted his touch made a red haze dance before his eyes. He wanted to plunge into the heat and warmth of her welcoming body. His jaw clenched as he fought for control.

'That's for me?'

'Always,' she agreed fervently, her back arching as he came over her. She tensed her body, half expecting to feel the thrust of him within her. The tantalising brush of his silky hardness against her soft belly made her cry out in exquisite frustration. She couldn't bear this any more; she needed him—she needed all of him!

This had to be special, careful; he had to stay in control. She was so delicate and small, yet the supple strength in her body was a revelation to him. To resist the impatient, erotic undulations of the body beneath him took every ounce of his will-power.

When his lips moved over the silky inner aspect of her parted thighs it was only his hands anchoring her hips that stopped her twisting away from him.

'Ethan, please!' she begged, unable to articulate the elemental needs his erotic caresses were building up. He ignored her soft cries and continued the relentless torment of her senses. The heat pooling in her lower body spread to her limbs, which felt so heavy she didn't think she could move them from the bed.

When he eventually pulled himself up the bed until they lay shoulder to shoulder she was half panting, half sobbing. His own features were taut and strained; his cheekbones seemed to be jutting sharply through the tightly stretched skin and beads of sweat stood out across his brow.

'I needed to taste you.' Apology, confession, challenge, it was all three.

Sensing he needed reassurance, she took his face in her hands and pressed her lips against his. 'I just need you—right now!' she added, her voice low and urgent.

Her back instinctively arched as she rose to meet the thrust of his body. Eyes tight closed, she waited, and when he did move she gave a shuddering sigh of relief as, by slow, sensual inches, he let her absorb all of him.

'Perfect, perfect, perfect,' she said as she pressed her open mouth against the damp skin of his corded neck. Her fingers kneaded the flesh of his shoulders as her body twisted experimentally.

'The rhythm was slow, slick and smooth; it fed the fire inside along with the frustration. Her hoarse, urgent appeals had a rather dramatic affect. One second he was careful, measured co-ordination and the next he was rampant, elemental urgency.

'You waited for me,' she said, some time later.

Ethan stroked her damp hair as she lay curled up, her face nestled on his chest. 'You noticed.'

'It wasn't the sort of thing a person misses,' she said with a sleepy yawn. 'You know, I've never woken up with someone in the morning. I wonder what it's like?' she mused.

'I'd imagine it rather depends on who you went to sleep with the night before,' he responded drily. 'Are you glad about this, Hannah?' His stroking hand hovered above her head as he waited tensely for her reply. The silence stretched, punctuated by the soft sound of her regular breathing. 'Are you asleep, Hannah?' he said sharply.

'I think so,' came the distinct response.

Ethan began to laugh softly.

'What's wrong?' She half raised her head but he pushed her back down.

'Nothing. Go to sleep,' he urged.

CHAPTER FIVE

'ISN'T this cosy?' Faith Kemp spooned some more sugar into her tea and looked around the table with warm approval.

Ethan, too experienced in his mother's brand of dry humour to be misled by the artless innocence of her comment, frowned.

'"Cosy" isn't a term I'd have thought appropriate for this room, Mother.'

A small frown pleated Hannah's smooth brow at his words; they carried a definite hint of wry criticism. Mrs Turner, on finding they had guests, had moved breakfast to the formal dining room. It was a charming room, and, with the French windows flung open onto the south-facing lawn, a person would have been hard-pressed to find a more elegant spot in which to dine, but Ethan was right: *cosy* it was not.

'I see your influence hasn't extended this far, Hannah,' Faith agreed. Her eyes went to the vases crammed with wallflowers on either end of the mantel-piece and she regarded her daughter-in-law with a shrewd expression that reminded Hannah uncomfortably of her son.

'You can't improve on perfection,' Hannah said quietly. And I can't compete with it or Catherine.

There was no doubt that Catherine had had perfect taste. Perfect taste, perfect body, perfect husband, and she, Hannah, was a visitor. It was a feeling she couldn't get rid of—she was a visitor in her own home.

'Is that why you haven't changed the decor? I was wondering—it was the first thing Catherine did when she ousted me.' Faith smiled at Drew and patted his hand familiarly. Hannah could see Ethan's knuckles grow white as he lifted his coffee cup. 'Personally I've never seen what's so tasteful about employing someone else to decide how your home should look. I always had a more hands-on approach myself. Could you be an angel, Drew, and pass me some of that honey?'

'You chose to go,' Ethan reminded her stiffly. 'And Hannah knows perfectly well she can do anything she wants to the house.'

'From the expression on her face I'd say she might have felt more comfortable if you had told her that, Ethan.'

Hannah didn't have time to alter her expression before Ethan switched his attention to her. She breathed a sigh of relief when Emma's voice diverted him.

'Will you take me to Louise's party today, Daddy?'

'That might be managed.'

'Louise has a nice house,' she mused, playing with a plastic cartoon figure she'd extracted messily from the bottom of a cereal packet. 'It's not as big as ours. Is that why her mummy and daddy sleep in the same bed?'

The stunned silence seemed to go on for ever.

Every one's a gem! Hannah swallowed a bubble of pure hysteria. She couldn't look at anyone, least of all Ethan. 'I'll just go and bath Tom,' she babbled, unstrapping the toddler from his high chair.

As she whisked him out of the room she heard Faith say with great panache, 'I'm sure Louise's daddy doesn't snore like yours does, Emma. Tell me, are grannies invited to this party of yours?'

Today, for the first time, Emma's words hadn't been

strictly true. The timing was ironic—the very morning after the night before! If only the childish curiosity had voiced itself when they'd been alone, or at least not in front of what had felt like half the county. Drew already thought they had a very weird relationship. Hannah gave a sudden laugh—they *did* have a very weird relationship!

Hannah sighed and trailed her fingers in the bubbly water of Tom's bath and smiled at his grave expression as he experimented with eating the bubbles.

'I could always have asked you to be my witness, couldn't I, champ?' she said, rubbing a sponge down Tom's back. After all, Tom had been in a perfect position to verify her sleeping arrangements when he'd slipped between their sleeping bodies that morning. He'd been surprised, but not displeased to find his father occupying the bed.

Ethan had glanced at the clock and groaned as he'd awoken with a toddler on his chest. 'Does he do this often?' he enquired, having coaxed his son under the blankets.

'Most mornings.'

'Good God!' Tom, unable to stay still for more than thirty seconds, bouncing on the bottom of the bed. 'We'll have to do something about this young man's body clock. This wasn't the way I'd intended starting the day.'

The quick glance from his eyes didn't speak of two-mile runs or aerobics. It spoke of things much more intimate and leisurely. Her skin began to tingle as heat surged through her body. For once they seemed to be on the same wavelength. Since she'd woken an hour or so earlier her imagination had been running rampant. Even with her eyes tightly closed she'd been able to feel the heat from his body, even though he'd shifted to the opposite side of the bed. The muscles of her belly had gone into spasm as she'd breathed in the musky, masculine scent of his skin.

As she'd stretched she was reminded of the previous night. Her body ached from the vigour of his possession. A possession that she could only view with a slightly detached sense of wonder this morning.'

'I should get up and warn Mrs Turner we have guests.'

'How could I forget?' he remarked drily. He didn't turn away as she clumsily struggled to cover her nudity with a thick, shapeless robe.

Hannah was relieved when he didn't comment on her self-consciousness. 'You must be pleased to see your mother.' Didn't he realise how lucky he was to have one? She was constantly amazed at how people took their families for granted.

'Do I detect a hint of disapproval?'

'Well, you weren't very welcoming to her.'

'I didn't feel very welcoming, and under the circumstances I think I was a paragon of restraint. Marriage!' he snorted. 'She must be insane.'

'She didn't want you to marry me either,' she reminded him. 'I overheard something she said,' she added as his brows shot up in surprise.

'But I did, didn't I?' he said softly, an indecipherable expression flickering briefly into his eyes. 'Don't worry, my mother isn't going to lose any sleep over my disapproval—any more than I do over hers, Hannah. She makes her own rules up and changes them when they don't suit her any more,' he said with disgruntled disapproval.

Hannah couldn't help smiling.

'What are you thinking about when you smile so secretively?' he asked, lifting an arm over his head and rubbing his tousled hair. He hardly looked like the same person as the sleekly suited sophisticated animal who left the house every morning. She loved him so much she wanted to yell it out loud; being a cautious girl, she didn't.

'You don't want to know.'

'Try me.'

Oh, I'd like to, she thought, watching the muscles of his shoulders tighten and relax as he moved his head to a more comfortable position. Rather boldly, she let her eyes drop lower to where the sheet skimmed his narrow hips. She was mildly shocked, and much more than mildly aroused by the direction of her thoughts!

'I was thinking genetics have a lot to answer for. You seem to be developing a talent for making rules and then changing them too,' she elaborated.

He got the message and an answering gleam of wry humour shone in his eyes. 'Is that the only talent you think I've got?'

'Everyone says you're an excellent barrister,' she remarked rather primly.

'I wasn't thinking professionally.'

'I don't know how to flirt,' she admitted as frustrated confusion closed in. It was hard to know where jokes ended and the serious stuff began. If she got caught up in this intimate repartee, she might just confess more than she wanted to. More importantly, more than he wanted to hear.

'I'm quite good at repairing gaps in education, if you'll let me.'

He wasn't laughing at her any more. Looking into his

compassionate, warm eyes, she wanted to blurt out the truth.

'I think you're *very* good,' she replied in a breathy, intense voice. 'I'd better go and catch Mrs Turner. Come along, Tom.' She caught the little boy by both hands and swung him off the bed. Sometimes, she reflected, it wasn't just what you said, it was the way you said it. No wonder Ethan was staring at her in that peculiar way!

'I'm sorry about that.'

Hannah started, and twisted around as the deep voice close beside her abruptly broke into her reverie. She inadvertently sent a shower of water over the front of Ethan's pale chinos.

'Sorry.' Flustered, she reached forward and dabbed at the damp spots with her wet hands, making matters worse.

'It doesn't matter,' Ethan choked hoarsely. Seeing her kneeling there had brought a vivid image of her sweet mouth…! He caught his breath as his body automatically responded to the provocative mental picture. He smiled in a strained manner as she looked up. If he answered the puzzled question in her eyes, she'd be shocked. Although she hadn't seemed shocked last night. Recalling the wanton eagerness of her responses wasn't the best way to dampen his arousal, he decided wryly.

'You should change them—not here,' she added hurriedly. Even if I am in a perfect position to assist you… What devilish imp planted that naughty idea in her head? It could have been worse—she might have said it out loud! 'I mean, you could if you wanted to, but I wasn't suggesting…' She took a deep breath. Best stop before she sounded like a total idiot. Who am I kidding? she thought. There's no *before* about it.

Ethan got down on his knees beside her. 'It might be simpler if I got down as you're so interested in the floor.'

'I lost something.'

'What?'

She eyed him rather resentfully; he wasn't being very helpful.

'Dog, Daddy,' Tom said, throwing a large duck at his father. Ethan ably caught it.

'Duck.'

'Dog,' Tom repeated with a grin.

'I get the impression Tom's vocabulary is a bit restricted.'

'He's very intelligent,' Hannah said, automatically defensive at any implied criticism. 'All animals are dogs and all men are Daddy.'

'I noticed he's indiscriminate with his favours when he attached himself like a limpet to Drew this morning,' Ethan observed drily.

'You're determined to dislike him, aren't you?'

Ethan was being so unfair. She could appreciate that the idea of your mother with a younger—a very much younger—man might be hard to take, but he wasn't even trying. 'Why can't a woman fall in love with a younger man? People don't have any control over these things,' she said indignantly.

'Don't mistake your own unrequited passion for Mother's affairs of the heart. She's never settled for unrequited in her life!' Ethan's lips formed into a hard line of disapproval.

'Oh!' she said without thinking. 'I forgot I told you that.'

'Well, I haven't forgotten,' he replied rather grimly. 'I've been thinking—it might be better, considering

Emma's comment, if we stopped having separate rooms.'

Hannah wiped her hands carefully on a towel. 'In the interests of keeping up appearances,' she said carefully.

'That's one reason,' he agreed blandly.

'There's another?'

'I want to make love to you every night and every morning and occasionally in between.'

The towel slipped unnoticed to the floor and Hannah continued to wring her hands, oblivious to the loss. 'Is that being a bit ambitious?' she asked huskily. In her wildest dreams she'd never imagined such an outspoken avowal of desire.

'Worried that I'm not up to it?'

'Well, there is a worrying age gap...'

'You minx!' he said, a hard light glinting in his eyes as he took her by the shoulders. 'There's no comparison and you know it. I'm really sorry if you were embarrassed downstairs, Hannah. Are you happy about last night?'

'I'm glad about last night, Ethan,' she admitted huskily.

'Out, Daddy, now!'

Ethan closed his eyes in exasperated defeat. 'That child has inherited his timing from his grandmother and her domineering disposition. I never seem to see you without the children being around.'

Hannah, who was feeling equally frustrated, tugged the chain on the bath plug with unwanted viciousness. 'What do you expect when you marry the nanny?'

Ethan didn't look too happy at being reminded about this. 'You're not the nanny now—don't you ever have any free time?'

'Nannies have free time, Ethan; I'm the wife. We

don't have a nanny.' She wrapped a fleecy towel around Tom, who, giggling, ran into the nursery.

'*My* wife.' The words emerged with a proprietorial vigour that stopped him short. Dear God, if he went on like this he'd be acting as if he was jealous of his own son. The idea of such pitiable behaviour made his nostrils flare in distaste.

Hannah saw his expression and immediately misinterpreted it.

'A fact that seems to make you ecstatic,' she flashed sarcastically. There was a real danger here that she would forget the simple fact of the situation. Ethan didn't love her.

'Last night...' he began.

'Oh, last night,' she said bitterly. 'I might be flavour of the month right now, but how long is that likely to last?' She voiced the fear that lurked uppermost in her mind.

'I can see you have high expectations.'

'Realistic expectations,' she returned, folding a discarded towel. She began to rise, but Ethan's fingers closed around her upper arm to prevent her.

'You expect boredom to set in?' he suggested, his jaw clenched in a fixed, humourless smile.

Hannah refused to meet his eyes. Of course he was going to get bored with her—it hurt, but she had to face facts and be practical. 'It's possible,' she muttered morosely.

'I think you'll find my imagination is up to the task of holding your attention for the foreseeable future,' he predicted arrogantly.

She let out a tiny startled shriek as she found herself suddenly flat on her back with Ethan kneeling over her. He thinks I'm saying I'm likely to be bored with him!

In a less tense situation this might have made her laugh, but laughter wasn't really appropriate.

As his arms slowly slid further away from her head his body dropped lower—so low that his chest almost touched the upthrust of her breasts, which rose in harmony with her erratic breaths.

'What are you doing, Ethan?' The sensual lethargy that was insidiously robbing her limbs of power had reduced her voice to a throaty whisper.

'Your comments seem to imply you have a low boredom threshold. I'm just trying my humble best to vary my technique.' His features were taut with barely repressed emotion.

'There's no need to take it personally,' she murmured, as he applied his mouth to the extended length of her throat. Her damp flesh where his tongue had touched burned and tingled. A reckless light blazed in the depths of his eyes and, hypnotised by the glow, Hannah couldn't look away. How had she missed the lethal, insolent sensuality in this man she'd married?

'Then I'm sure you won't take this personally, will you?' he drawled, placing a kiss on the tip of her nose. 'Or this?' This time he caught her chin. 'As for this…'

As his teeth nipped her full lips Hannah's mouth opened, and he took immediate advantage of the fact, plunging deeper into the warm, moist sweetness within. All Hannah was conscious of in that moment was the skilful thrust of his tongue and the hard pressure of his lips; nothing else existed. Her fingers sank into the lush thickness of his dark hair and she moaned softly as her body stirred restlessly.

'I can vary it, and I do detached and objective as well as impersonal.'

Hannah blinked, unable quite to bring his face into

focus. 'No, thank you. I think you've proved your point. Will you let me up? I have to go to Tom.'

She felt somewhat ambivalent when he immediately rolled away from her and stretched out beside her on the floor. 'I know, but do you *want* to?'

With trembling fingers, Hannah refastened the two top buttons of her shirt. 'I want...' she said, sitting up and looking down at his prone body. 'I want to...' Tongue caught between her teeth, she placed her palm flat on his chest. 'I want to carry on kissing you.'

What reckless, self-destructive impulse had induced her to say anything so stupid? She didn't wait around to see what Ethan made of this confession—she scrambled hurriedly to her feet and fled into the nursery.

When, a few minutes later, Ethan followed her, he just stood silently watching her dress the squirming youngster.

'Aren't you neglecting your guests?' she asked, when his silent presence had stretched her nerves to breaking-point.

'I didn't invite them,' he reminded her caustically.

'That's no excuse for bad manners,' she snapped, as he dropped in her lap a sock Tom had flung across the room.

'Not trying to get rid of me, are you?'

'Whatever gave you that idea?'

She gave a sigh of relief and buried her head in Tom's hair when Ethan decided quite unexpectedly to leave. What had she started? she wondered with apprehension. And, more importantly, where was it going to lead?

'Where's Emma?' Ethan asked as he walked into his study to find his mother calmly leafing through his address book. 'Anything I can help you with?'

'No, I've got what I want, thank you, Ethan,' she said, untouched by his sarcasm. 'And Drew has taken Emma down to the river to feed the ducks. Now I come to think of it, I think she took him,' she mused. 'A forceful child.'

'It didn't occur to you I might not want my daughter to wander around in the company of a total stranger?'

'Drew is not a total stranger.'

'To me he is. You'll have to pardon me if I don't find your character reference comforting. You can be as irresponsible as you like about your choice of friends, Mother, but when it comes to my children—' He drew a sharp breath of displeasure. 'It's bad enough that I have to stomach the man under my roof. Which way did they go?'

'I wouldn't know, darling. Before you go,' she said, picking up the telephone, 'you didn't have any plans for tonight, did you?'

Ethan paused in the act of leaving, a suspicious frown on his face. 'Why?'

'I thought it might be nice to invite a few old friends round tonight.'

'I was hoping for a quiet night—'

'Don't be such a bore, darling!' she chided briskly. 'You'll be old before your time. I've already spoken to Delia,' she expanded.

'Who is Delia?' he asked in confusion.

'Your housekeeper.' She shook her head at her offspring's obtuseness. 'And she's quite happy with the idea. She's recommended some caterers. Naturally I'll invite some of your friends too.'

'That won't be necessary, Mother.'

'It's no trouble,' she assured him. 'I've already spoken

to that nice secretary of yours and she's ringing round
for me.'

'You rang her at home?' He shook his head in disbelief. 'You're impossible!'' he growled. 'Do as you
like,' he said, wiping his hands of the whole affair.

'I knew you'd like the idea,' she said imperturbably.

'Just a small party—forty or so.'

Hannah blinked as her mother-in-law placed a friendly
arm around her shoulders. '*Tonight?* Isn't that short notice? Perhaps some people won't be able to come,' she
suggested hopefully.

'Oh, everyone accepted.'

'I'm not sure Ethan—'

'Oh, Ethan was very enthusiastic about it.'

'He was?' Maybe it was his lack of confidence in her
own abilities as a hostess that made Ethan normally veto
any large gatherings. 'What shall I do?'

'Don't worry about that; everything is in hand. What
are you going to wear? That red dress you had on last
night was quite charming. I hope you've got a few more
like that in your wardrobe. I want to show you off to
my friends.'

'Hannah, whose head was spinning, thought it was
time to get a few things straight. This was the same
woman who had begged her son not to marry her;
Hannah had heard her with her own ears.

'I thought you didn't like me. You didn't want me to
marry Ethan.'

'Quite right, but that wasn't because I didn't like you.'

'Then why...?'

'I knew Ethan didn't love you, and in my view marriage with love is hard enough, but without it...' She
lifted her shoulders expressively. 'I could also see you

loved him.' Her blue eyes grew compassionate as she watched the colour flee dramatically from Hannah's face. 'I didn't want to see you hurt.'

'Did you tell Ethan?' Hannah asked, as her heart continued to hammer sickeningly. She couldn't bear the humiliation if he'd known all along. No, he couldn't have, she reasoned. If he'd even suspected how much her heart had been involved in her decision to accept his proposal, he'd have run a mile.

'What a silly question!' Faith's clear, amazingly youthful laughter rang out. 'I knew he was acting out of concern for the children. Catherine's death was a terrible blow for him; he hadn't recovered. I know he didn't turn to the bottle or neglect his work, but he was hurting more than anyone guessed.'

Not more than I guessed, Hannah thought sombrely. She didn't need anyone to explain to her how unemotional Ethan's motivation for marrying her had been. It was something she was reminded of in a hundred little ways every day.

'I can see now that you've helped him recover.'

'I haven't done anything!' Hannah protested, embarrassed by the warmth of the other woman. Faith was in danger of overestimating Hannah's influence—she'd probably read all sorts of things into that embarrassing but unrepresentative scene she'd witnessed the previous night. Ethan's recovery had more to do with the resilience of his character than anything Hannah had done. Whilst he might be inexplicably sexually attracted to her, she hadn't heard, or expected to hear, a single word of love on his lips.

'You've loved him,' Faith said warmly, 'and as his mother I can only thank you.' She linked her arm with Hannah's and they walked out onto the terrace. 'This view is the one thing I really miss about this house,' she confessed, inhaling the heavy fragrance of the autumn day. 'It's so *English*. It makes me feel quite nostalgic, but then it isn't raining. I find it hard to be nostalgic about rain.'

Hannah, who loved the smell of wet leaves under her feet, just smiled. 'Didn't you mind when your husband left the house to Ethan?' she asked curiously. The idea of leaving this house, even after the short time she'd lived here, was horrifying.

'Not in the slightest. Jordan knew I never felt the same way about this place as he did. We were two very different people, she reflected, a wistful expression drifting over her face. 'We both made a lot of concessions to make our marriage work. I certainly wouldn't have stayed in one place for thirty years for anyone other than Jordan. I doubt if he'd have gone trekking in the Himalayas for anyone but me.'

'And now you've met someone else,' Hannah said quietly. She was deeply touched by this glimpse of a profound love. It was the sort of love she'd always dreamt of.

'Ethan told you that, did he? Yes, I'm very lucky.'

'But it's not Drew, is it?' Her feminine instincts told her Ethan was wrong.

Faith threw back her head and laughed. 'Of course not.'

'Then why did you tell Ethan that it was? He's really upset about it.'

'I didn't tell Ethan; I just didn't correct him. My son, Hannah, has a tendency towards pomposity, and I feel it my maternal duty to pull him down to size occasionally.'

'Who is Drew?'

'Drew is soon to be Ethan's stepbrother.'

'You're marrying his father!' Hannah cried, unable to repress a chuckle at the joke. She suddenly let out a sharp cry as a red-hot needle of pain bit deep into her shoulder. 'Something stung me,' she explained, rubbing the area, which was already beginning to puff up.

'It looks like the sting is still in. We'd better do something about it immediately.'

Hannah was rather glad she'd weakly allowed herself to be flattered into purchasing several more outfits when she'd bought the red dress. This full-length cream slip dress, which her mother-in-law had heartily approved of, was made of soft, clinging silk. She hadn't expected an opportunity to wear it to present itself so soon.

When Hannah had worried about the puffy, discoloured area around her bee sting Faith had produced some antihistamine tablets, which had taken down the swelling miraculously.

Hannah touched the single string of luminous pearls that hung about her neck as she descended the sweeping staircase. Ethan's mother had dismissed Hannah's reluctance to wear them the way she steamrollered any obstacles.

'Beautiful.'

Pausing on the bottom step of the stairs, Hannah turned around with a smile. 'They're Faith's.'

'I didn't mean the pearls,' Drew said, stepping through the library door. He was pulling at the folds of his tie with a dissatisfied frown. 'I meant the neck. Damn thing—I should have left it the way it was.'

'Can I help?' she offered with an amused smile. Drew looked grateful.

'Help away.'

'Do you always carry a dinner jacket in your ruck-sack?' she teased, adjusting his tie and retreating up one step on the staircase to view her work. 'That's better,' she approved, stepping down the step again and flicking a speck of dust off his lapel.

'Faith arranged for someone to pick one up from my flat.'

'You live in London?'

'Split my time between London and New York.'

'Would I be wrong to assume your work normally involves wearing a tie?'

'I went into the family firm.'

'So what does that make you when you're not being a beach bum?'

'Would you believe a banker?'

His self-conscious grin was contagious, and Hannah found herself laughing back. 'Then why the worn den-ims and rucksack?'

'Would you believe a woman?'

'It must have been serious,' she said sympathetically.

'She got cold feet the night before the wedding.'

'Ouch! Should I ask why?'

'I was too boring. She thought my suit would need to be surgically removed by the time I was forty and I lacked spontaneity. She did go into more detail than that, but I won't bore you.'

'So you turned your back on your suits.'

'I gave most of them to a charity shop, actually,' he recalled with a wry smile. 'That was twelve months ago. I was backpacking across South America when my dad decided enough was enough. We were still discussing the issue, quite loudly as I recall, when Faith appeared. She took on the role of referee as one born to it.'

'And they fell in love. That's so romantic!' she breathed.

'Just how many people have you invited, Mother?'

Unconsciously Hannah's fingers tightened on Drew's jacket lapel as she heard Ethan's voice. 'I've hardly seen Ethan today,' she said, as her stomach began to perform painful contortions. She swallowed hard to relieve the sudden constriction in her throat.

'I suppose it depends on why you're trembling as to whether I'm envious of him or not.' Drew grimaced as she cast a reproachful look at him. 'Sorry,' he murmured pacifically. 'It's probably my fault—he's been shadowing me in case I pocket the silver.'

Hannah winced. 'Sorry,' she said softly. Ethan was going to be mad when he realised how far out his first impressions had been.

'Thirty or so of your *closest* friends! I thought this was going to be a quiet dinner party.'

'Don't fuss, Ethan. We only managed to contact fifteen of yours. Here's Hannah and Drew—what a charming picture they make. Don't you think so?'

Under the ferocity of her husband's regard, Hannah realised she was still clutching at Drew's lapel. Her hand fell away self-consciously.

'Charming,' Ethan drawled. 'Where have you been hiding today?'

Hannah's temper rose at the accusatory note in his voice. 'I could ask you the same question, except I already know. Drew has told me. Do yourself a favour and reduce the surveillance, Ethan, he's not marrying your mother. You may be a great legal mind, but right now you're just in danger of looking rather silly.' Ignoring the shocked look of outrage on his face, she sailed past him, head held high.

The guests, as was often the case, arrived in a deluge,

rather than drips, and Hannah was saved from listening to the scorching response to her reckless words that she was certain Ethan had composed.

He'd deserved it, she decided, flicking a covert glance to the opposite end of the room where he was laughing at something Miranda had said. *She'd* obviously been ready to drop everything at short notice in order to make Ethan laugh. Laugh—I'd like to make him plead for mercy, she thought viciously, draining her glass of wine.

Bringing his mistress into this house, flaunting her under my nose, she silently fumed, ignoring the fact that Ethan was a very reluctant host. How dare he humiliate me?

'Are you feeling all right?' a voice at her elbow enquired.

She turned to find Drew regarding her overbright eyes and flushed cheeks with a doubtful frown. 'You're a man.'

Drew agreed nervously with this accusation. In his experience, conversations that began like this were apt to get uncomfortable.

'Do *you* think she's beautiful?' Hannah demanded. She tossed her head in the direction of the tall redhead. 'Of course she is,' she replied, without waiting to hear his opinion.

'So are you.'

'You're such a *nice* man,' she said, regarding him affectionately. 'You'd never invite your mistress to a party at your wife's home, would you? No, of course not, you're far too consid…conside…thoughtful.'

'I think there's a possibility you're jumping to conclusions here,' he murmured, removing the empty glass from her limp grasp. 'Just how much have you had to drink?'

'Not enough!' she informed him darkly. 'Can you

dance? I can't. You could teach me...' she announced, smiling at this inspired idea. She swayed closer and wound her arms around his neck.

'*I'm* more than capable of teaching my wife anything she needs to know.'

Hannah pulled in the opposite direction as she was pulled from one pair of masculine arms to another. 'I prefer to dance with Drew,' she said haughtily, pushing her hands against Ethan's chest.

'Will you lower your voice?' Ethan said from between clenched teeth as he favoured her with a furious look. 'People are staring.'

As Ethan stepped into the slowly moving throng, Hannah felt the inevitable magic of his touch taking over. She wanted to be angry, she wanted to hate him, but how could she when her whole body was gently throbbing? The strength of his big body, the musky, warm scent of him overlaid by the elusive fragrance he sparingly wore—it all conspired to bewitch her senses.

Throwing her head back, she saw the muscles clench beside his stern mouth as she deliberately plastered herself against the hard length of his body. Well, what did he expect? Was she supposed to stand back calmly and watch him flirt so outrageously with *that* woman? No, it was about time she asserted herself, and if he didn't like it—tough!

'What do you think you're doing?' he asked hoarsely as she reached up and wound her fingers in dark strands of his hair.

She pouted consideringly and regarded him through half-closed eyes. 'I haven't decided yet. Doesn't Miranda dance?'

'You're drunk!' he accused.

'As a matter of fact I've only had two glasses of wine.

I do feel a bit odd, though,' she confessed as she noticed
the room beginning to spin faster than she was.

'We should get out of here.'

'You're ashamed of me!' she accused, standing stock-
still. She put a hand to her head. 'I feel a bit...' She
swallowed as beads of sweat broke out over her upper
lip.

'Ethan, dear,' Faith said a little nervously as she appeared at his elbow, 'Drew said Hannah was feeling a
little unwell.'

'I'm not drunk, Faith. Tell Ethan I'm not drunk.'

'The thing is, I think this might be my fault.'

'I hardly think so, Mother, unless you've slipped her
a Mickey,' Ethan said tersely.

'Not exactly, but I did give her one of my antihistamine tablets for that bee sting she had this afternoon,
and I forgot to mention they don't mix too well with
alcohol.'

Ethan closed his eyes and swore softly but compre-
hensively under his breath.

'You can't talk to your mother like that, Ethan,'
Hannah protested.

'I think we should get you out of here.'

'Unilateral decisions!' Hannah said, wagging her finger admonishingly in his face. She took him off guard
as she pulled free of his supporting arms. 'Oh, dear,' she
whispered as her knees began to buckle. Just before
Ethan caught her, she asked the question that was uppermost in her mind.

'Is Miranda your Friday night, Ethan?' Call it acous-
tics or bad luck, but her voice carried clear as a bell
from one end of the room to the other.

CHAPTER SIX

'How are you feeling now?'

'If you ignore the headache and the fact a sip of water makes me feel sick, I feel great. Who took my clothes off?' Hannah felt the bed give as Ethan sat down on it.

'Me.'

'I suppose you were there when I was sick too.' Could this humiliation get any worse? she wondered glumly.

'Yes.'

'Oh, God!' she moaned 'I want to die.'

'You mentioned that too. Life will probably look more appealing after you've slept some more.'

Hannah didn't reply, because she knew it wouldn't. Once she was better she'd have to face the full force of his anger and contempt. Selective amnesia would have been nice, but she could recall in horrifying detail every syllable and every sultry pout her lips had formed. There was a strong possibility she could never appear in public again without a brown paper bag over her head. The story of Ethan Kemp's mad, drunken wife would probably become legendary in the rarefied legal circles that Ethan inhabited.

Just thinking about it brought her out in a cold sweat. She'd humiliated and embarrassed him in front of his colleagues and friends. How he must regret the day he'd married her. Tears seeped from under her closed eyelids and ran slowly down the curve of her cheek. She could taste the saltiness as they touched her dry lips...

When she woke again, Hannah did feel a lot better.

Her head felt muzzy and her stomach a little delicate, but other than that things were back to normal. She sat up and gasped. Not quite normal—Ethan didn't normally sleep in her bedroom armchair.

He was sound asleep. His head was thrown back, one of his hands brushed the floor and one knee was hooked over the armrest. The chair was much too small to accommodate his bulk.

Holding her breath, she tiptoed across the carpet. She almost tripped over his crumpled jacket and tie. Through his white shirt she could see the shadow of dark body hair. Sleep softened the lines of his strongly sculpted features; he looked younger—not exactly vulnerable, but softer. She clasped her hands together to resist the impulse to stroke back the hank of dark hair that flopped in his eyes.

He shifted slightly and she held her breath. She became suddenly conscious of the fact she was wearing only a pair of silky pants. If he woke up now and she was caught in all her voyeuristic glory...! With one last covetous look at his sleeping figure, she crept away. Taking great care not to make a sound, she closed the bathroom door silently behind her.

By the time the room was filled by warm steam she was starting to feel more human. She might even be able to take his justified anger. Yelling at a semi-comatose victim couldn't compare with the pleasure of telling a conscious culprit exactly what he thought of her. Not being able to shout at her last night had probably only concentrated his sense of outrage, she concluded gloomily.

If only her lowered inhibitions hadn't brought her submerged jealously so visibly and audibly to the surface. The last thing she could remember before she'd passed out was Ethan's face, white with fury. He didn't flaunt his emotions for the public, and he hadn't needed to spell out the fact that he expected her to emulate his flawless public behaviour. Ethan Kemp's wife did not dance on table-tops and definitely didn't accuse her husband of infidelity!

She still revolved under the warm spray when some sixth sense told her she was no longer alone. It was only a hand across her lips that stopped her screaming. His face wasn't furious this time, more broodingly angry. Anger wasn't the only emotion revealed as the water streamed over his face. She contemplated the hungry, restless look in his eyes with breathless shock.

'I didn't want you to bring Lancelot in here with your screams,' he said, removing his hand from her lips. 'You appear to arouse the chivalrous instinct in my soon to be stepbrother. I suppose you were in on that little secret?'

Obviously I don't have the same effect on you, Hannah thought. She wanted to back away but she was rooted to the spot as firmly as a rabbit caught in the headlights of a car, her fate just as inevitable as that creature's. As Ethan's glance dropped insolently over her slim body, it was almost as if he was daring her to object to his presence.

'I don't think it was meant to be a secret, exactly.'

'I recognise the hallmarks of my mother's twisted sense of humour.'

'Well, at least she has one.' Oops, that had just sort of slipped out. 'You'll get wet if you stand there,' she added shakily. The rolled-up cuffs of his white shirt were already damp, his tanned forearms gleamed with moisture and the steamy heat clung to his hair as tiny, silvery water droplets. 'If you thought I'd scream, why did you creep up on me?' I hope his watch is waterproof, she thought, fretting over this irrelevant detail.

My God, he was impressive enough to take the most objective observer's breath away, and she was a long way from objective! She knew there wasn't an ounce of surplus flesh on his taut, lightly tanned body. Long and lean, with just the right degree of muscle definition, he was the closest thing to male perfection she'd ever seen. If he weren't dressed, what would it feel like to run her hands over his slick skin? She could imagine the sharp contraction of those strong belly muscles and the deep quiver of his thighs. The water ran into her open mouth and she nearly choked.

He observed the minor convulsions with a disturbing smile. 'You want exclusive rights in the surprise department, do you? Isn't that just a bit unreasonable?' He found great difficulty in tearing his eyes from the way the water reached the uptilted peak of her small breasts and then cascaded down the sharply defined valley in between.

Hannah watched in confusion as he closed his eyes and slowly shook his head from side to side. She gasped as, with his eyes still shut, he stepped fully clothed into the cubicle and closed the door behind him. He threw back his head and let the water run over his face. As she watched, the white material of his shirt became transparent, and she could see the clear outline of his muscled torso and the curling shadow of his dark body hair.

'What are you doing?' she asked hoarsely.

'My spine's all tied in knots—a nice hot shower should do it some good.' Now he had his eyes open she had the distinct impression he wasn't missing any detail of her naked body. Unconsciously her chin went up as she met his sensual appraisal head-on.

Those knots couldn't be as complicated as the ones that tightened in her belly. A space that moments before had seemed luxurious was now overwhelmingly claustrophobic.

'Fully clothed?'

She couldn't do anything but stare as he unfolded her fingers one by one from the bar of soap she clutched. Her hands were hardly adequate to cover her growing sense of vulnerability, so she kept them rigidly to her sides. Wondering just what he was going to do next made the blood pound in Hannah's ears.

'Not an insurmountable obstacle. I was hoping my wife might give me a hand. Such a delicate, pretty hand too,' he murmured, turning her hand palm up and pressing it to his lips.

'I suppose you're pretty angry with me?' she said faintly. This was probably part of some elaborate punishment, she thought hazily.

'Why should I be angry?' he enquired, evincing confusion. 'Oh, you mean because everyone knows my wife thinks I have a mistress. And the fact I've had to offer the woman you so publicly slandered a grovelling apology. You've managed to destroy my respectable image with remarkable efficiency.'

She watched as, very slowly, he worked the soap into a lather. Ethan looked at his soapy hand, then into Hannah's wide eyes, and deliberately closed his hand over one taut breast. A deep sigh rippled through his body. 'Like lovely firm tender apples, ripe for the plucking,' he breathed, leaning forward to plant his other hand on the tiled wall behind her head. His thumb moved back and forth over the erect nipple.

'Ethan!' she gasped. Was he trying to say he wasn't having an affair? she wondered, too intensely involved with the movements of his clever, cruel hand to concentrate properly on anything else.

'That's my name,' he agreed grimly, 'and don't you forget it. Not Jean-bloody-Paul, and not Drew what's-his-name. Ethan Kemp, your husband, the man who shares your bed, given the opportunity. Why I let you turn this house into a damn hotel, I don't know.'

'This isn't a bed.'

'Don't be pedantic, Hannah.' He took her chin in his hand and stroked her jawline with his thumb.

'I'm sorry. I...I assumed... I mean, you're a normal man with the usual appetites, and she's attractive, clever...'

'You assumed one hell of a lot. And it didn't bother you when your fertile imagination decided I'd been sharing more than professional courtesies with the nubile Miranda.' He sounded strangely annoyed by his interpretation of her reaction.

'It was none of my business.'

'That's not the way it sounded last night. It sounded like it bothered you a lot.'

'Things are different now...' she said, feeling trapped by his relentless pursuit of her motivation. She could hardly say, I'm jealous as hell because I'm in love with you, could she?

'At least you admit that much,' he grated triumphantly. His kiss was tinged with a driving desperation, and he sucked at her mouth as if he'd drain her. Hannah's hands opened and closed spasmodically as her fingers twisted the fabric of his shirt-front.

She could hardly breathe. His expression was hidden by the mist that filled the small cubicle. 'Your clothes will be ruined,' she reminded him as his hands ran slowly over her from shoulder to flank, turning her body into a quivering mass of burning anticipation.

'To hell with my clothes.'

Considering his lack of concern, it was with a clear conscience that she tugged urgently at the front of his shirt.

'Oh, yes,' he approved throatily as she touched her tongue experimentally to the pebble-hard centre of his male nipple. His fingers pushed roughly into the saturated strands of her hair. Encouraged by his response, she suckled softly. Under his open shirt her arms moved around his waist, drawing her breasts closer to his lean body. She leant into him, revelling in the strength of his muscular thighs which were braced to support her body.

'You like it?' she gloated. Delight and a heady sense of feminine power coursed through her veins as she shook the wet hair from her eyes and gazed up into his face. He liked it—it wasn't hard to interpret that strange mixture of pain and pleasure in his short, irregular gasps and the ripples of muscular contractions that ran beneath the smooth surface of his golden skin.

Drops of water trembled on the tips of her eyelashes and she licked at the moisture that ran into her mouth. Deliciously confident, she reached up to ease the clinging material off his shoulders.

This was a Hannah she hadn't known existed: a sexy, irresistible Hannah. Men were putty in her hands—Ethan was putty in her hands. Maybe not putty—Ethan felt altogether too firm to be classified as malleable, and certain parts of his anatomy were anything but soft. The shirt fell in a sodden heap on the tiled floor and she spread her splayed fingers up over his taut belly and across his chest and shoulders.

'You are so beautiful!' she breathed almost reverently.

'Do it again!' he commanded hoarsely. 'I want to feel your mouth on me.' A harsh cry was wrenched from his throat as she eagerly complied.

Abruptly his hands slipped under her bottom and he lifted her to waist-level. Hannah's legs automatically wrapped themselves around his waist as he walked forward with her until her back was pressed against the tiled wall.

Hannah didn't respond passively to his initiative. She matched the hungry ferocity of his mouth, and the fine, rhythmic rotation of her pelvis drove her closer to him, and drove him beyond reason. Ethan was gasping and groaning as he continued to feed on her lips frantically. He backed out of the shower cubicle and, without lifting his head from the sensual feast, carried them as far as the bed. The metal frame hit the back of his legs and he collapsed backwards with her onto the sheets which still bore the earlier imprint of her body.

Hannah let out a startled cry as she found herself lying on top of him. She sat upright and wiped away some of the wetness from her face.

'The other night was the first time for me in more than three years.'

Hannah stared at him. It wasn't a joke; he meant it! Her instinctive response of smug elation was swiftly followed by the sobering realisation of the reason for his abstinence. The memory of Catherine had been more important to him than the needs of his body. That memory still hung between them, a constant reminder of the contrast between their places in this household and in his heart.

'Would you have been happier if I'd kept a mistress? You don't look very pleased.'

'I'm wondering what's changed. Sex wasn't in the forefront of your mind when you married me.'

Ethan's eyes, dark with passion, moved slowly over the slender, pale curves of her body. 'It is now,' he groaned, reaching for her.

Hannah might not have been satisfied with the absence of an adequate explanation, but in every other way she was totally satisfied!

It began with a cushion lobbed at her from the trio involved in an enthusiastic game on the floor, which involved Drew on all fours, with Tom on his back, being chased around the room by Emma. Hannah's retaliation escalated things to the point where they were all on the floor, panting and laughing as cushions were flung back and forth.

'This will all end in tears,' Hannah predicted as she held her arms across her face to hold off a vicious onslaught from her stepson.

'Being struck repeatedly over the skull by a soft object is the very latest cure for a hangover,' Drew teased softly. 'Surrender?' he suggested in a louder voice.

'Never!' she cried, flinging herself sideways to catch a stray missile. Her retaliatory strike went wildly astray and hit— The room went suddenly silent as they all saw whom it hit.

Miranda Saunders was standing in the doorway beside Ethan. She was casually dressed, but desperately elegant, and Hannah was immediately conscious of her own deficiencies: namely a face pink from exertion and hair which looked neither smooth nor sleek. Dressing for comfort rather than glamour no longer seemed the best decision she'd made today. Brushing down her crumpled clothes, Hannah got to her feet.

'We were…' she began breathlessly.

'It looked like great fun,' the redhead responded with a tentative smile.

'I see your head is quite recovered, darling,' Ethan drawled as she tried to press her tumbled locks back in place. 'Miranda dropped in to see how you are.' He responded to the appeal in Hannah's wide, horrified eyes with a casual and, to her mind, deeply callous smile. 'I'll chase up some coffee for you both. Perhaps we should transfer this rough-house out into the garden. Do you play soccer, Drew?'

Typical—he could make out they were bosom buddies when it suited him! Hannah thought with disgust. She watched the traitors respond eagerly to Ethan's suggestion. He can't do this to me—he *is* doing this to me, she realised bleakly.

'Girls can't play football,' she heard Drew observe with innocence as they left the room.

'Tell him, Daddy!' Emma shrieked, tugging her father's arm. 'Tell him I can.'

'Show him, sweetheart,' she heard Ethan advise as he closed the door firmly behind them.

'I had to come.'

To watch me grovel, Hannah thought weakly. To grind her elegantly shod size six into my face. 'About last night…' she began. There was no point skirting around the issue.

'Are you feeling better?'

'I stayed in bed until midday.' Even in the midst of her present predicament she felt something warm and heavy stir in the pit of her belly as she recalled with whom she'd stayed in bed most of the morning. That memory's not going to help you now, she told herself sternly.

'I owe you an explanation.'

Hannah blinked in bewilderment—either she had missed something or they were talking at cross purposes. Her bewilderment wasn't diminished by the embarrassed expression in the tall young woman's eyes.

'You do?'

'I've no excuse. I knew he was married.'

Hannah froze. What was she saying? Had her first instincts been correct? Ethan had denied it and it hadn't occurred to her to disbelieve him. Had he sent Miranda in here to flaunt their affair as some sort of bizarre punishment? She cursed her willingness to accept everything he said at face value as a tide of bitter humiliation rose in her throat.

'He's so attractive, but I don't need to tell you that.' Miranda's smile was apologetic. 'He was very kind to me, which makes it worse, really. He's such a good teacher.'

Don't I know it? Hannah thought grimly.

'I pulled out all the stops to get him.'

And what man could resist what this woman had to offer? Hannah thought grimly. What man would even try? Not my husband, obviously. The pain solidified in Hannah's chest until she felt as if she couldn't breathe. All that stuff about it being the first time in over three years and she'd swallowed it whole.

'At first he ignored it,' Miranda recalled, her colour heightened. 'Then when I got a lot more obvious he told me straight—he told me he wasn't interested. He was very convincing,' she recalled drily. 'When you go after what you want,' she observed philosophically, 'you have to take the rough with the smooth, but that's part of being a woman today.' She sighed. 'I may be tough, and not as moral as I should be, but I do have a conscience.

So when I realised last night that you thought...' She lifted her slender shoulders and her face twisted in a grimace of self-contempt. 'I couldn't bear it if I was the cause of any conflict. He obviously loves you very much.'

These revelations left Hannah's thoughts in a mad whirl. Ethan had refused this gorgeous creature! Only for a split second did she contemplate that he had done so because of her. In her heart she knew that it was Catherine's image which gave him the strength to resist temptation—that and the fierce sense of protectiveness he felt for his children. She couldn't afford to nurture any illusions on that score; he'd protect this marriage because it gave the children stability.

'You didn't have to tell me this,' she said wonderingly. She didn't think she'd have been brave enough to do so if the circumstances had been reversed.

Miranda nodded slowly. 'I know—maybe I'm not as hard-boiled as I thought,' she mused with a self-conscious laugh. 'I don't usually go after married men. I had heard some gossip that your marriage wasn't all it...' She cleared her throat noisily. 'Not that that's any excuse,' she said hastily. 'And I can see it wasn't true anyway. You must think I'm a total bitch,' she said frankly.

'I don't know what I think of you,' Hannah said honestly. 'I know it must have taken guts to come here and say this.'

'I turned the car around three times on the way over.'

'I appreciate your honesty.' It was hard not to, and she could afford to be generous, she told herself, under the circumstances. 'And I can understand any woman finding Ethan irresistible—I do myself,' she admitted, with the faintest glimmer of a mischievous smile.

Miranda gave a sigh of relief that was half a sob. 'Thank God,' she breathed. 'I thought you might want to…'

'Tear your hair out?' Hannah suggested. 'The thought did occur to me.' It wasn't easy to make a joke out of the violent revulsion of her feelings.

'Miranda gone?'

Hannah turned from her task of preparing vegetables to look at Ethan in a manner as casual as his own. 'I couldn't persuade her to stay,' she quipped waspishly.

'Pity.'

'A real loss,' she drawled. 'Did you enjoy your game of football?'

'Emma has a very pronounced competitive streak,' he mused, rubbing his shin. 'Just like her…'

'Like her mother,' she finished emphatically, even though the reminder hurt.

'I was gong to say like me,' he said, his brows raised a little at her tone.

Her sensitivity had made her jump the gun, and she continued swiftly to extinguish that disturbingly thoughtful expression on his face. 'I'm glad you tell her she can do anything she sets her mind to,' Hannah observed truthfully. 'It's important for any child, not just a girl, to have someone believe in them.' She was unaware of the hint of wistfulness that had entered her voice.

'Did nobody ever believe in you, Hannah?' he asked softly.

She gave him a startled look. 'Are you trying to discover the reason behind my inadequacies?' she asked sharply, instinctively reacting to the pity she thought she read in his voice. 'Just because I can't ride or sail or swim like a fish—swim at all, actually,' she corrected honestly, 'it doesn't mean I don't have self-confidence. When you're on your own you learn a lot about yourself, about your own resources. Don't worry, I won't infect Emma with my lack of self-esteem.'

'Where the hell did that come from?' he asked incredulously when she paused, breathless and flushed. 'Why the hell should I give a damn if you can ride or...? Oh, I see, you think I'm comparing you to Catherine.'

Everyone else did; why should he be different? 'It must be impossible not to,' she observed gruffly.

'You're two very different people.'

'I know that. *She* didn't need a prenuptial agreement,' she snarled, throwing down the knife in her hand. She stopped, appalled at what she'd just said. Why, she wondered with despair, do I keep saying these things?

'The circumstances were very different when I married Catherine. You could say I learnt from experience,' he added obscurely. 'Surely what we have now is more important. I enjoy being with you, Hannah; I *enjoy* you. I think you enjoy me.'

The soft way he emphasised 'enjoy' brought a rash of goosebumps to her warm skin. 'Why? Why do you...enjoy me?' she asked, unable to tear her eyes from the warmth of his regard.

'You...' he began emphatically. He stopped, and she had the impression he was backtracking. 'You make me laugh,' he finished lightly.

Hannah sighed softly. The sense of anticlimax was intense, but she was prepared to accept the pace he set. Slow and steady got there in the end, and she really did feel now that they had a destination to reach together. 'Like a clown?' she suggested.

'Like a warm, funny...lady.'

This time it was Hannah who felt things were running

too fast. The glow in his eyes made her knees tremble. 'You no longer appear to think Drew is a danger to the moral fibre of this family.'

Ethan acknowledged her withdrawal with a wry quirk of one darkly defined brow. 'I must admit it's easier to view him in a kinder light now I know he's not sharing my mother's bed.'

'You're so broad-minded!' she admired with a twinkle.

'Although my good opinion does depend on how often I find him wrestling on the floor with my wife,' came the surprising response.

Glancing up at his face, Hannah couldn't decide whether he was joking or not. 'The children were there,' she reminded him with a scornful laugh.

'That doesn't alter the fact he was enjoying himself far too much.'

She judged this an excellent time to divert the conversation. 'I hear you've been the victim of sexual harassment in the workplace.'

'A sad statistic,' he agreed with sigh. 'Why are you peeling these, anyway?' he asked, biting into a chunk of crisp carrot. 'What's happened to Mrs Turner?'

She sharply tapped the back of his hand as he attempted to filch another. 'This is therapy. Did you know what Miranda was going to say?'

Ethan shrugged. 'Not word for word.'

'I suppose you think I should admire your self-restraint?' she said, running the peeled vegetables under the cold water.

'Not really. I've never been an advocate of mixing business and pleasure. I've seen too many romances between colleagues go sour.'

'I didn't think there were enough women to go

around,' she responded waspishly. The implication that he might have accepted Miranda's overtures if they'd met under different circumstances really made her hackles rise.

'Did I say all those relationships needed one of each sex?' His grey eyes sparkled with amusement at her shocked expression.

'I thought *our* relationship was a business one,' she challenged, responding to his patronising amusement with belligerence. She always felt at a disadvantage when something reminded her of how unsophisticated she must appear in his eyes. 'We've got the contract to prove it.'

'Marriage lines—most people have those.'

'I was thinking more of the prenuptial agreement I signed in triplicate.'

'Does it bother you that much? You didn't have any objections at the time.'

'I appreciate you have to protect yourself against gold-diggers.'

His brows drew together at the bitterness in her voice and his grey eyes raked her face with a shrewd expression. 'You're far too naïve to be a gold-digger.'

'Is that a criticism?' she snapped.

'An observation. I know you a little better now than then.'

'Carnally, you mean, I suppose?' She literally bit her tongue—she sometimes forgot that Ethan was an expert at making people say things they didn't intend to. His clever mind made thumbscrews obsolete.

'That too,' he agreed. A tiny shiver ran down her spine as she intercepted the sensual appreciation of his narrowed glance. 'Did you know you just put the peel

in the pan and the potatoes down the waste disposal?'
he enquired with interest.

'It's a new recipe.'

His lips twitched but his expression remained solemn.
'The results should be…interesting.'

'Actually, I'm quite a good cook. I've never been able
to afford expensive ingredients but I learnt all the basic
techniques.'

'You're very quick at getting the hang of…''basic
techniques''. It's something I noticed straight away.'

The innocent expression in his eyes didn't fool her for
an instant. 'If you don't believe me, I'll prove it to you.
I'll cook you dinner.'

'I do believe you, but I accept the offer,' he responded
promptly. 'We'll make a date.'

'Well, that should give me a good couple of months
to prepare,' she observed drily.

'Are you suggesting I neglect you?'

'I don't need entertaining.' She bit her lip—the last
thing she'd wanted to imply was that she felt like a neglected wife. Their relationship might have changed, but
not that much. 'I just think you work too hard.'

'Maybe you're right,' he mused thoughtfully. 'Can
you be free for a couple of hours tomorrow morning? I
needn't be in chambers until after lunch.'

'Why?'

'Wait and see.' He helped himself to another piece of
raw carrot and she could see she'd have to be satisfied
with these enigmatic words.

CHAPTER SEVEN

'WHO lives here?' Hannah asked. Ethan had explained that the Palladian mansion they had entered had been divided into four palatial apartments.

'A friend.'

The door opened onto a vast, modern, furnished open-plan living space. 'An unmarried friend,' she observed, looking at the monochromatic decor, leather and chrome. Someone who didn't feel the need to remain faithful to the period feel of the house, obviously.

'How did you know?' Ethan asked curiously.

'It might as well have a notice saying "Boy's Room",' she whispered, touching the sharp corner of a head-high metallic sculpture. 'Whatever gave you the idea I'd want to visit your friend, Ethan—especially one with such a questionable taste in art?' Was this his idea of a treat?

'Don't worry, he's not at home.'

'Then why are we here?'

'Come this way and all will be revealed,' he promised enigmatically as he caught hold of her hand.

Trotting to keep up with him, Hannah allowed herself to be led over acres of deep white carpet and down several shallow flights of stairs to wide double doors, which Ethan opened with a flourish.

'Wow!' she said, blinking.

'What do you think?'

'I think it's decadent and splendid,' she breathed. 'I sort of expect to see Roman ladies...' she said softly, looking around the mosaic-tiled pool room with wide-eyed appreciation. With the gentle trickle of the waterfall and the ceiling-height frescoes, it was all incredibly over the top.

'Slipping off their togas—you see that too?'

She laughed at the lascivious grin on his face. 'Why did you bring me here, Ethan?'

'Why does a person usually come to a pool? I'm going to teach you to swim.'

'No!' she said, shaking her head from side to side. 'I can't...'

'Nonsense!' he said bracingly.

Easy for him to say, she thought resentfully. 'It sounds like you're of the "throw 'em in the deep end" school of thought. We had a teacher like that at school—I was his Waterloo.'

'Don't be such a defeatist, Hannah. Everybody should learn a basic skill like swimming. You want to set a good example to the children, don't you?'

'That's moral blackmail!' she accused.

'If it works, who cares?'

'Not you, obviously. I can't swim; I don't want to swim.'

'Why?'

'I'm scared,' she burst out. 'There, satisfied? Go ahead and laugh at my athletic incompetence. I'm a physical coward—always have been.'

'Cowards don't throw themselves out of moving vehicles.'

'That was desperation, not bravery.'

'I know you're scared,' he said calmly, placing both his hands flat on her shoulders. He wasn't laughing at all. 'I'm with you; you don't need to be frightened. I won't let anything hurt you.'

It was foolish to read anything deep into his calm words, but she couldn't prevent the warm glow of pleasure that instantly filled her.

'I'll make a fool of myself.'

'You'll have fun.'

Hannah glanced at the glittering depths lit by a very elaborate display of underwater lights. 'I suppose you think I'm a wimp?'

'Don't tell me what I think,' he said firmly, patting the side of her nose.

'I don't suppose Catherine was scared of anything.' She could have screamed with vexation as the words slipped out. It hadn't been her intention to flaunt her insecurities. She could almost hear him wondering how to be tactful without telling huge whoppers. She couldn't imagine he'd be pleased at the implicit invitation to massage her ego.

'We're all scared of something.'

'I know—in this instance, water. Nothing you can do is going to make me brave and fearless.' Or give me long blonde hair and legs that end at my ears, she added silently.

'Do you think I'm trying to turn you into a Catherine clone?' A frown wrinkled the wide sweep of his brow. 'Is that what you imagine this is all about?'

'I think you're too much of a realist for that,' she replied bluntly. Her eyes slid away from the suspicion in his, because his words had exposed some of her very real fears. What did they have in common other than the children? The answer to this question was all too obvious—nothing. Right now he found her a novelty, but today's joke would become tomorrow's embarrassment and he'd start trying to change her.

'Don't say I didn't warn you,' she muttered, when his

regard and her own gloomy thoughts became too uncomfortable. 'I suppose there are swimsuits here somewhere?'

'Afraid not. You have to remember this pool was Adam's ultimate seduction device. Swimsuits would have ruined the ambience, from his point of view,' he added virtuously. 'Myself, I find the idea of peeling away those scraps of clingy Lycra quite...stimulating.'

'You're degenerate,' she said firmly. 'And as for the man who lives here, he must be pathetic.'

'Not pathetic—a professional bachelor, who, alas, is no more.'

'He's dead?' Hannah said, shocked by his callous attitude.

'Married,' Ethan corrected mournfully. He ducked as she aimed a blow at his head. 'For some reason his wife refused to live here,' he observed with wicked laughter in his eyes. 'Strange girl. He's altered beyond recognition these days—she's even weaned him off the Mickey Mouse ties. The flat's in the hands of an agent and we have permission to use it.'

'I suppose you said you wanted somewhere private for your...your...'

'I told him I wanted to teach my wife to swim. Adam's bed does everything short of play the national anthem, and personally I find gadgetry a little distracting. Besides, I've got a perfectly good bed at home.'

'I can't swim without clothes,' she said firmly.

'That's where you've been going wrong—you'll find it much easier without them,' he promised.

'What are you doing?'

'Taking my clothes off.'

'I can see that.'

'I think it must be a gender thing. You wouldn't find a man asking totally irrelevant questions.'

He was completely unselfconscious about his body. Lips slightly parted to draw air into her tight chest, she watched the muscles of his strong back ripple as he bent to kick off his shoes. His clothes were folded into a neat pile and his moleskin trousers slid to his feet. He stepped out of them.

Turning around, he made it clear for the first time that he was well aware of her interested gaze. She gave a small sharp inhalation as he removed his boxers.

'When the shutters are down you have very articulate eyes,' he said by way of explanation, before he turned and dived into the water, his body hardly creating a ripple. He took a couple of lazy strokes before he slid beneath the surface. After a moment's panic she could see him moving.

The condition of his body had made it starkly obvious what he thought her eyes had been saying. The idea that he had been privy to her erotic fantasies as she'd admired him brought hot colour to her cheeks.

As much to divert her thoughts as anything else, she peeled off her clothes swiftly, leaving them in a crumpled heap. Unlike Ethan, she walked around the perimeter to the opposite, shallow end of the pool. She kept on her bra and pants which, she reasoned, covered more than most swimsuits.

She was standing with her toes barely covered by water on the top step when Ethan's dark head emerged from the water several feet away. He waded towards her.

'Coward!'

'I told you I don't like water. I'm cold,' she complained.

'Cold? I have it on the best authority that this place

is kept at a constantly humidified heat of eighty-four degrees. Actually, I was referring to your outfit.' He shrugged as he examined the white cotton broderie anglaise set. 'Maybe it'll make it easier to concentrate on the task in hand,' he conceded.

Hannah shivered again. She wasn't proof against the erotic movement of his hips as he surveyed her through half-closed eyes. 'Nothing will make this easy,' she muttered as she eased her way to the next step.

'Take your time.'

'I've every intention of—' She let out a shrill cry as she lost her footing. 'Ouch!' she gasped as she landed on her bottom. The sudden realisation that water was lapping past her middle made her stroke out in panic.

'Calm down, no damage done.'

Panic receded but Hannah remained tense and suspicious. 'It wasn't your behind that cushioned the fall,' she grumbled feelingly. Ethan's grin was very white and shockingly heartless.

'Come on, take my hands. What's wrong? Don't you trust me?' He looked boyishly injured at the idea.

'Now you come to mention it...' she said slowly, not impressed by his act. Tentatively she reached across to bridge the gap between them. She was genuinely terrified of water. Logic told her she was perfectly safe, but logic didn't prevent the adrenaline being pumped in massive quantities around her body. Her heart was beating so hard she felt physically sick.

'Go on—the first step's the worst.'

He was right, but the second and third weren't much better.

The first time, half an hour later, she put her head under the water she emerged breathless but triumphant.

'I did it!' She flung her arms around Ethan's neck and kissed him firmly on the lips.

'If only all my students showed their gratitude so nicely.'

'How many other women have you taught to swim?' She let her hands rest loosely on his shoulders and very daringly let her feet float gently off the floor. Ethan's wet skin had a gorgeous rich texture.

'I haven't taught you yet.'

'You didn't answer my question.'

'You noticed that, did you?'

'Why do you have to talk like...like a lawyer?' she sniffed.

'I am lawyer.'

'Feeble excuse.'

'Have you had enough for one day?'

'Probably,' she confessed.

'But you enjoyed it. Admit it, Hannah.'

'Sort of, once I relaxed a bit.'

'I'll have a quick swim whilst you get a shower.'

She was rather disappointed; she'd half expected the intimacy of the occasion and the setting would have led inevitably to a less businesslike encounter. But it would seem the only thing he'd had in mind was teaching her to swim. She watched for a moment as Ethan lapped the pool with slow, effortless elegance and then did as he suggested.

Whilst she was still combing her damp hair she heard him turn on the shower. She squeezed the excess moisture out of her wet underwear and took one last glance at her reflection before making her way back to the pool edge, to wait for him there.

'You're looking a bit warm,' Ethan observed, leaning on the back of her lounger.

Hannah opened her eyes and found herself looking up into his face. 'This place must cost a fortune to heat,' she said, dabbing the slight film of moisture over her upper lip with the tip of her tongue.

Ethan caught her elbow as she got to her feet. 'I've been thinking about getting one at home. What do you think?'

'Isn't that a bit extravagant?'

'I think the budget might stretch.' His teasing wasn't of the unkind variety, but Hannah immediately felt gauche and awkward.

'I forget sometimes,' she murmured as they retraced their steps through the flat.

'What did you forget?'

'That you're rich. I expect that sounds stupid to you, but watching the pennies is sort of an ingrained habit with me.'

'How old were you when your parents died?'

'I never knew my father, so I suppose he might still be out there somewhere. Mum died when I was four and I went to live with my gran. I went into care when she had a bad stroke.'

'It must have been tough.'

'I'm tough.' Her frown didn't invite sympathy; it wasn't intended to.

'I'm beginning to realise that.' The quiet reticence had been all he'd seen for a long time, but now he wondered how he had missed the delightful complexity of this young woman. He'd hardly noticed at first that when they disagreed over something to do with the children, although she listened to what he said, somehow he usually ended up agreeing with her without quite knowing how it had happened.

Her recent, more overt rebellions had been impossible to miss, and very taxing on the nerves, but he had to admit they hadn't been boring. Hannah was one book with a very deceptive cover, and, like any good book, once opened almost impossible to put down.

'My survival instincts are pretty well developed.' She was glad of the autumnal chill in the air outside; it cooled her overheated body.

A gardener was working in the communal grounds, collecting the fallen leaves. Ethan called out a greeting to him as he opened the car doors.

'Is that why you married me?'

Hannah blinked in shock as he slid into the car beside her. 'I... I... Why else?' She affected a casual shrug, but the question had really shaken her.

He'd never come right out and asked her before. She'd thought it hadn't mattered to him so long as things were going as he wanted. Was it because he wanted different things now, or did he suspect? The truth had been trembling on the tip of her tongue. She flicked a curious look at his profile. What would he have said if she'd told him the truth?

'Do you mind?' she couldn't stop herself asking.

'Mind the fact you married me for purely practical reasons? Why should I? Under the circumstances it would be a bit hypocritical. If you'd been like Patricia I'd never have suggested it.'

'Who's Patricia?'

'The one in between Sophie and Rebecca,' he said with a frown of concentration as he recalled the roll-call of previous nannies.

'What did Patricia do?'

'Followed me around with big spaniel eyes,' he recalled with a shudder. 'She could always find an excuse to knock on my door in the middle of the night dressed in floaty, transparent things.'

'You mean the poor girl had the bad taste to fall in

love with you.' Thank God she had managed to bite back
the truth. The idea of him thinking about her like that
left a bitter taste in her mouth.

'Love! I doubt that. Infatuation, possibly.'

'I'd have thought worship would have been a positive
attribute in a prospective bride.'

'Under the circumstances, hardly,' he said with a grimace of distaste.

'You mean she'd have expected you to make love to
her?' Hannah suggested. Her chin was tilted at a bellig-
erent angle as she turned to glare at him. 'How perfectly
horrid for you. Sleeping with the nanny!' she mocked.
'Whatever next?'

The heaving indignation was not wasted on Ethan.
'It's plain ridiculous to compare yourself with what's-
her-name, and you know it. So don't get all uppity with
me.'

'From where I'm sitting the similarities jump up and
hit you in the face.'

'Did *you* expect me to make love to you?'' he shot
back.

'No!' Dream, crave and yearn for it, yes. Expect, no!

'Exactly,' he replied triumphantly. 'You didn't marry
me thinking I could walk on water either.'

She could say no in all honesty to this. In her case
love hadn't been blind, just reckless! 'I didn't hold it
against you that you couldn't.'

'You're generous to a fault,' he agreed drily. 'Seriously, it would have been a disaster to enter into a marriage with some starry-eyed female who needed constant
reassurance. Perhaps more marriages should be based on
friendship.'

'We weren't friends,' she reminded him uncoopera-
tively. What female with blood in her veins would have

been co-operative in her place? she thought indignantly. He had some hide, singing the praises of platonic marriage when everyone knew he'd been crazy about Catherine! He'd had it—why should he imagine she didn't want the opportunity to experience the wild impracticability of mutual love? Was she being unreasonable and greedy wanting more?

'But we are now?'

If she'd been standing on the particular rug that question had pulled from under her feet, she'd have been flat on her back. Fortunately she was enclosed by soft, supportive leather upholstery which cushioned the impact considerably.

'I...we...possibly,' she finished lamely. She ought to be glad he thought of her as a friend. Only his words triggered a seething sense of dissatisfaction.

'That's what I like to hear: an unequivocal endorsement. Let's skip over the friends bit. We're lovers, or aren't you sure about that either?'

'I'm not in the witness box,' she retorted. Just as well too, considering!

'There was no compulsion...'

Speak for yourself, she thought, quashing an alarming desire to indulge in hysterical laughter. 'Compulsion' summed up her feelings for this man pretty well.

'Nothing forced,' he continued persuasively. 'It was a natural progression...spontaneous. What,' he enquired icily, 'is so funny about me being spontaneous?'

'It's just not a term I associate with you.'

He gave her a second suspicious sideways glance before returning his attention to the road ahead. 'Neither of us had any expectations and things just progressed naturally. We're not in love, but it doesn't make the physical aspect any less fulfilling. I think things have turned out very well.'

Maybe he was right, she reflected. He looked a lot more relaxed than she'd ever seen him before. Perhaps sex without the unstable element of love was less fraught. Who was she fooling? Deep down she knew she couldn't have slept with him if she hadn't been in love with him; it was an integral, inseparable part of the equation for her. Men were obviously different.

'Shall I take your silence as agreement, or should I start to worry?'

My God, I could tear his comfortable appraisal to shreds with three little words—three little words I'm not going to use. He'd never know how bitterly ironic his cutting assessment of the lovelorn nanny was.

'If propinquity and convenience were all that mattered, surely most men would sleep with their secretaries.' She pursed her lips reflectively. 'Maybe most men *do* sleep with their secretaries.'

'Obviously I find you attractive.'

'It's not obvious to me.'

He dismissed this statement with a sceptical smile. 'Would you have married me if you'd found me physically repulsive, no matter how attractive the package I offered you? I don't think so.'

'Correct me if I'm wrong, but the logical progression of that argument seems to be that if I'd been a real dog you wouldn't have popped the question. Your frankness has a unique charm all of its own, Ethan.' Whilst she didn't expect to be romanced with sweet nothings, this was stretching her tolerance to breaking-point. 'And it would be a mistake to assume that, just because you're a pin-up, all women feel sexually attracted to you. Women are not as predictable as men.'

'Have I said something to annoy you, Hannah?'

'Whatever gave you *that* idea?'

'I thought you'd appreciate candour. Or are you still miffed because I didn't make love to you back at the pool?'

'My God,' she breathed, her bosom heaving, 'when they handed out ego you got a double dose.'

'You were expecting me to.'

'I was not!' she lied firmly.

'I thought you might think the setting a bit too... obvious.'

'You're so sensitive.'

'I'm glad you appreciate the sacrifice,' he replied with cheerful unrepentance. 'It *was* a sacrifice.' This time there was no humour in his voice. 'When you look at me with those big, hungry eyes I personally couldn't give a damn about the decor.'

'I don't have...' She couldn't bring herself to say 'hungry eyes'.

'Are those sweet little cotton things in your bag?' He moved his hand from the gear lever to flick the handle of her leather bag and she nodded vaguely, her head still spinning. 'So you're wearing what, exactly, under those?' Briefly his glance flicked over the russet cotton sweater and above-the-knee black skirt she was wearing.

She glanced down, just to check the lacy top of her hold-up stocking wasn't showing. Her heart was beating slow and strong and she was conscious of every separate thud.

'Nothing would be my guess,' he said thickly. 'You'd better come clean because I have every intention of finding out for sure when we get home.'

The mental picture that accompanied his words breached her feeble mental defences and robbed her body of strength in one fell swoop. 'Don't I have any say in the matter?'

'The idea excites you as much as it does me.'

'How do you know?' She plucked at the stretchy fabric of her sweater, as it showed an unfortunate tendency to cling to the visible proof that supported his theory.

'I know—the same way I know it's my face you see when you close your eyes when I'm making love to you. My face—not some shadowy figure you still harbour romantic fantasies about.'

'What are you talking about?'

'You told me about your unrequited love. Did you forget?'

Lies had a way of catching up on a person! I really don't have a good enough memory to lie effectively, she thought, trying desperately to recall exactly what she had said.

'I don't want to talk about it.' Did I give this face-saving device a name? she wondered. She racked her brains and still couldn't recall.

'Do you feel guilty because you enjoy it when we have sex? Do you feel you're betraying your love?'

Hannah raised her eyes from her stubborn contemplation of her clasped hands. Was this a classic case of transference? Was that actually how *he* felt when he made love to her?

For some reason he was working himself up into a real temper. One glance at his rigid profile told her that.

'Imaginary lovers are perfect, but bloody unsatisfying. I may not fulfil the criteria of all those mawkish romances you read, but I do assuage your needs,' he assured her with arrogant confidence.

She dismissed the possibility that the idea of her fantasising about another man whilst she was in his arms

was fuelling his antagonism. He had no reason to be
jealous of her love; he didn't want it himself. He'd spelt
that out pretty clearly.

He was also as wrong as he could get about the criteria. He filled all the criteria of dream lover—all except
one: he didn't love her to distraction.

'Perhaps the difference is we don't make love, we
have sex.'

'I haven't noticed you complaining.'

'I've got lovely manners.'

'I used to think so...' He switched off the engine as
they drew up outside the stable block and gave her the
benefit to his full attention—something she found hard
to bear. 'Will your lovely manners make you feel
obliged to agree when I suggest we go indoors and
"have sex"?' There was no missing the irony in his
voice.

'No.' She reached out and touched the side of his hard
jaw. He turned his head and pressed his lips to her open
palm. 'But wanting to touch you will,' she confessed
huskily.

Hot satisfaction flared in Ethan's eyes, and without
saying a word he got out of the car and tore around to
the other side with flattering speed to open her door.

'It's not very practical with a houseful of people,' she
said regretfully. Already aroused, she was filled with
writhing frustration by the knowledge that this verbal
foreplay was going nowhere.

'If you had a spontaneous husband that might be true,
but you have me. I've planned meticulously for this
eventuality, and we have the place to ourselves for the
next two hours at least.'

She gaped at him incredulously, but he was too busy

being distracted by the length of leg she exposed whilst climbing out of the car to notice. 'You planned...?'

'Always be prepared,' he intoned piously. 'The boy scouts had a profound effect on my development.'

'I doubt very much if they had anything like this in mind.'

'And if my house weren't filled to overflowing with strangers,' he responded, sweeping her unexpectedly up into his arms, 'I wouldn't have to go to such elaborate lengths to get my own wife alone.'

'Your mother isn't a stranger, and Dre—'

'Shut up. I don't want to talk about my mother.' He proceeded to tell her what he *did* want to talk about, and Hannah was happy to listen.

Hannah got back home a little after seven. Faith and Drew had left that morning so, after the children had gone to bed, she and Ethan would have the whole evening to themselves. The first time since... Her cheeks flushed with pleasure as she recalled this new and exciting phase in their relationship; this wondrous circumstance was never very far from the forefront of her thoughts.

The passing days hadn't diminished her sense of wonder at the joys of intimacy. Where it would eventually lead them, she didn't know, but for once she was inclined to feel optimistic.

Perhaps it was even the time to admit to him her feelings. She had to tell him before they became too transparent to disguise. Would the gift of her love be something he appreciated? That was the troublesome million-dollar question that made her break off humming the cheery tune under her breath and begin chewing her upper lip.

He had certainly thawed out a lot during the past days, and not just with her. Although he hadn't gone so far as to laugh at his misinterpretation of his mother's matrimonial plans, she had got the impression his wry sense of humour had eventually appreciated the situation. He'd gone along with the proposed family get-together with his prospective stepfather with every appearance of approval, and he and Drew both seemed ready to accept that their mutual first impressions had been wrong. When Ethan capitulated, he did it in style.

Hannah was still on a high, and all things felt possible—even telling her husband she loved him! The afternoon had really boosted her confidence. Jean-Paul had arranged an informal meeting for her with the head of the French department. In retrospect it had been lucky he'd given her such short notice—she hadn't had time to talk herself out of it, or see problems where there weren't any.

It had all been very encouraging, and she'd been bubbling with enthusiasm when she'd stopped off at the pub for a drink with Jean-Paul and his wife, who was on maternity leave from her teaching post in a local secondary school.

The kitchen was empty, so she assumed Ethan was upstairs getting the children ready for bed. She looked at her reflection in a large gilt-framed mirror before going upstairs. The girl with the flushed cheeks, bright, shiny eyes and glossy hair looked unfamiliar to her; it was an image she would like to get used to. She was just straightening the neck of her red chenille jumper when Ethan's voice made her spin round.

'Hello!' she said back, hurrying forward. 'Where are the children?' she asked as she walked into the room and looked around with a puzzled frown.

'Ah, the children,' he drawled. This was Hannah's first inkling that something was amiss—seriously amiss. A sick feeling of dread began to churn in her belly. 'They're in bed.'

'It's early.' Her voice faltered as she met the searing contempt in his grey eyes. 'Is something wrong, Ethan?' Had she been wrong when she'd thought he'd accepted the fact that she wanted to further her education in the future? What else could explain the waves of hostility he was emanating?

'You can ask me that?'

'I don't understand...' His blighting anger seemed totally out of proportion to anything she had done.

'Where have you been?'

Hannah blinked. He must have got her message. It was Mrs Turner's day off, but Alexa had offered to look after Tom and bring Emma home from school. Alexa had been in the room when Jean-Paul had rung, and, much to Hannah's surprise, she had offered to look after the children. Hannah had hoped it meant a slow easing of hostilities.

'Not any local hospital—I tried them.'

'I went to the university and then I stopped for a drink with Jean-Paul. Alexa knew—'

'I'm well aware you dumped Tom with Alexa—it was she who contacted me after the school rang to tell her nobody had picked Emma up. I'm curious,' he said with biting sarcasm. 'Did you genuinely forget, or did you just assume somebody else would shoulder your responsibilities because you couldn't be bothered to spoil your fun? I know you left the university hours ago—I rang.'

Hannah was shaking her head slowly from side to side. He couldn't believe she'd actually desert Emma. The thought of the little girl waiting for someone to collect her, watching all her friends go home, brought a lump of emotion to her throat.

'Was she very upset?' How *could* Alexa use a child to drive a stake between her and Ethan? My God, she must really feel threatened, Hannah thought. She must really hate me!

'And am I to assume from the husky catch that you give a damn?'' he jeered. 'All you had to do, Hannah, was pick up a phone and Alexa would have collected her. But no, you couldn't be bothered even to do that! If the teacher hadn't been alert she might have tried to get home alone. A little girl, lost, alone, a soft target for any sickos out there.'

Her eyes darkened with horror at the picture his words painted. 'Alexa...'

'Alexa was worried sick. I said I'd ring her when you got back.'

Hannah caught his arm. She couldn't believe this was happening. God, what a fool she'd been to take Alexa's overtures of friendship at face value! 'You don't understand, Ethan. Alexa *offered* to look after Tom and pick up Emma.'

His eyes flicked dismissively over her face, icy with contemptuous disbelief. 'What reason would she have for lying? When I asked her to look after the children next week— Oh, yes, I'd planned to take you away,' he said, as she stared at him uncomprehendingly. 'It was meant to be a surprise. New ring, new start!' He extracted a small velvet box from his pocket and pulled out a gold ring. He flung it viciously across the room. 'Not only did you fool the children, you fooled me with your gentle, caring air. You've shown your real colours now, so don't try and shift the responsibility to someone else.'

'I'm not. She hates me!' Hannah cried, willing him to believe her. 'She thinks I've stolen Catherine's children, her home and...' she swallowed the aching constriction in her throat '...and you.'

Ethan laughed; it wasn't a pleasant sound. 'You're not the children's mother and never could be. A mother doesn't walk away from a child who needs her!' His voice shook with outrage, and his hand came down to cover like a vice her pale fingers that curved around his forearm. 'As for this house; you're the hired help here. The only thing that ever made you a possible mate in my eyes was the fact the children adore you and you're a competent nanny. I now discover that you're not even that!'

She recoiled from the undisguised contempt in his voice. He was trying to hurt, and, by God, he was succeeding! 'So now you don't trust me to look after the children?'

'Now I know you'll always put your own pleasure first. Now I'll make damned sure they don't suffer because you're a selfish little bitch. They don't deserve that again!'

As his lips compressed she could see a bloodless white line around his mouth. Hannah had reached the stage where his words hardly mattered. Her pain had reached saturation point; she couldn't hurt any more than she already did.

'If Emma and Tom didn't love you so much you'd be out of that door tonight! I've been inclined to dismiss the things Alexa has told me before as the concerns of an overprotective grandmother. I now see she was right about you all along.'

'What about us?'

'Us? There is no us.' He pulled her hand from his sleeve as if the contact offended him. 'As you pointed out, I'm a healthy man with needs and you were convenient.'

'It was more than that,' she protested. She couldn't let him reduce something that had been so fine and special to a sordid level.

'Believe that if it makes you feel better.' His amused contempt was like a slap in the face.

Ethan turned away abruptly; the sight of her bewildered, distressed face hurt too much. He couldn't let himself be sucked in again. 'Did you enjoy your evening?' he rasped sarcastically. 'Was it business or pleasure, or just a convenient combination of both?'

'Ethan!' She had to try and get through to him one last time. The sight of his broad, uncommunicative back was eloquent enough to tell her that her efforts were wasted. 'You find it incredibly easy to believe badly of me,' she accused.

What he'd find 'incredibly easy' would be taking her in his arms and kissing her. He despised himself for wanting to. 'The facts speak for themselves.'

There speaks the lawyer, she thought with a sudden surge of anger. Why was he doing this? She'd never given him any cause to think she'd neglect the children, and yet he'd tried and sentenced her before she'd even said a word. Anger she could understand, but his reaction seemed out of proportion. When he wouldn't look at her, she moved so that he had to.

'Things aren't always what they seem,' she challenged.

'*You're* not. You want to go to university and you don't give a damn about how it affects anyone else! We've just been a convenient stepping-stone for you.'

She gasped at the sheer injustice of this. She'd spent most of the afternoon trying to work out how and when she could begin a course without disrupting their family life. 'It's all right for you to work all the hours God sends, but if I want to do anything it's selfish. Their mother worked, didn't she?' No woman could run a business and take part in sport at the sort of level Catherine had without a co-operative partner.

'We're not talking about Catherine!' he snarled.

Something in his expression made her wonder for a split second if that were entirely true. Had everything in the garden been as perfect as everyone told her? The notion was banished as quickly as it had come. She was just clinging to comforting straws, like any other soul going under for the final time.

'When my children need me, I'm here. After your behaviour today I'm surprised you can fling around a word like "selfish" without choking on it.'

'Well, I hope *you* choke on the truth when you finally realise what a fool you're being right now!' she cried, running from the room.

She paused on her way back to her own room to look in on the children. They were both asleep. Looking at Emma's sleeping face, she couldn't comprehend how anyone could put a child in danger. Ethan had been right—she might have wandered off. She was only a baby, after all. Hannah was tenderly stroking a lock of golden hair off the childish brow when some sixth sense told her she wasn't alone.

Ethan was standing in the doorway, watching her. Silently their eyes locked. Defiance was the only thing that kept Hannah's tears at bay. As she brushed past him she could smell the alcohol he'd obviously just swallowed, but she was helpless to prevent her response to his closeness, that warm rush that unfurled in the pit of her belly and the light, dizzy sensation in her head.

She closed the door quietly behind her. 'I see now that it was a mistake overstepping the boundaries of my job description. I take it you have no objections if I take the nanny's bedroom in the future. I'll move my things back tomorrow.'

He didn't object, but then she'd known he wouldn't. He'd made it quite clear that as far as he was concerned there was nothing special about what they had together.

CHAPTER EIGHT

EMMA was so excited she hadn't slept the night before. Hannah knew because she had shared the little girl's bedroom in the hotel suite.

'Yes, you look lovely,' Hannah said as she finally secured a blue ribbon in the silk locks. 'Bridesmaids don't bounce.'

'They don't?'

'No, they glide elegantly.' Hannah demonstrated, swaying her hips in a lazy, exaggerated fashion.

'Exactly like a princess.'

'Will we be going soon?'

'I hope so,' said Hannah with feeling. Getting the child to the church before the flowers in her hair curled up and died, or something indelible and probably noxious got spilt down the front of the pink satin, had taken on the aspect of a nightmare.

'The car is here. You look spec-tac-u-lar!' Ethan said, sweeping his daughter high into the air. Ethan didn't comment on his wife's outfit.

Hannah knew she was looking drawn; over the past six weeks she'd lost weight she couldn't afford to. The muted grey and blue striped silk suit didn't totally disguise this fact. 'Shall I get Tom down?'

'No,' Ethan responded curtly. 'You take Emma.'

Hannah wondered how much longer she could take the constant slights before something cracked. Pretending to be part of a happy family was killing her

150

by slow, painful inches. 'Come along, darling. We can't keep Grandma Faith waiting—it's her big day.'

The car was waiting outside the hotel foyer. The doorman ushered them solicitously towards it. A sudden gust of wind lifted her hat and Hannah let go of Emma's hand to catch hold of it.

It all happened so quickly, she never did know what caught the child's eye on the opposite side of the busy road. One minute she was standing beside Hannah, the next Hannah saw the heels of her shiny new shoes and a fluttering pink hem.

With a cry of warning Hannah ran out after her, hardly noticing the sound of horns in her ears. She felt as if her feet were made of lead as she desperately tried to propel herself forward. Panting, she picked the child up from behind as she simultaneously became aware of the fact that she couldn't move fast enough to avoid the metal monster bearing down on them. It was instinct rather than conscious thought that made her throw the child clear just before everything went black.

Those ten minutes before the ambulance arrived were the longest and most nightmarish Ethan could ever remember. The hotel manager had proved to be a pillar of strength and calm. Ethan had been able to leave the children safely in his hands, knowing that his mother would come the instant she got his message.

Why wouldn't anyone tell him anything? They'd shut him out of the emergency room. He ripped the white rose from his buttonhole with an expression of disgust and ground it into the floor with his heel. Nobody came near the tall figure conspicuously dressed in the morning suit; he presented a daunting picture.

Standing in the glass revolving door with Tom in his

arms when it had happened, he'd seen everything. From a position of complete helplessness he'd watched it all. He'd seen the car hit Hannah and heard the sickening thud as her limp, apparently lifeless body struck the metal before sliding to the floor. The image was scorched in his brain.

'Mr Kemp? Would you like to come this way?'

The white-coated figure led Ethan to a small, impersonal office.

'Well?' Ethan didn't bother hiding his impatience. He was wound up tighter than a spring and it showed. His knuckles cracked as he flexed his long fingers.

The doctor didn't take offence at the aggressive tone; he'd seen and heard it all before. All the same, whilst quite a few of his customers might have liked to rip him limb from limb as the bearer of bad tidings, most of them didn't look capable of it. This one did.

'Your wife has been remarkably lucky. There's a hairline fracture of the temporal bone.' He touched his finger to the side of his head to indicate the position. 'That should heal with no ill effects. She is badly concussed but she did regain consciousness for a short time. I was honest with her when she asked me.'

'Asked you what?' Ethan had slumped into a straight-backed chair. The tension had drained from his body so abruptly, he felt as weak as a baby. She was going to live. Whether he had prayer, luck, or modern medicine to thank didn't matter to him—*she was alive*. Things were going to be different, he swore to himself.

'About the baby.'

'Let me get this straight,' Ethan said in a strained voice. 'My wife is pregnant?'

'*Was* pregnant.'

Ethan's head dropped forward onto his chest. 'Oh, my

God!' he said softly. He caught his head between his hands and rocked forward, his elbows clamped together.

'You didn't know? I'm sorry. It was very early, and there's no reason you can't have a healthy baby in the future.'

'Can I see her?' His complexion was tinged with an unhealthy pallor as he raised his head.

Numbed by having been overexposed to too much pain and suffering, the young doctor found his compassion unexpectedly stirred by the bloodshot, red-rimmed eyes of the man opposite him.

'Of course, but it might be quite a while before she wakes.'

The total amnesia only lasted for a few terrifying seconds. 'Mr Kemp?' she whispered in relief as the man seated beside her bed lifted his head. For some reason the man flinched as if she'd struck him.

'So you're back with us, Mrs Kemp?' The nurse hid her surprise at the formal greeting between husband and wife behind a professional smile.

Hannah remembered everything then—it was like walking into a solid wall. 'Ethan.'

'You're awake, Hannah.' Stating the obvious gave him a breathing space. It had been impossible to miss the grief of knowledge that had rushed into her eyes, only to be supplanted by a vague, distant expression.

'My head hurts,' she said dully.

'You fractured your skull.'

'I didn't mean to let go of her hand.'

Ethan looked at her blankly.

'Emma. She really is all right, is she? The doctor said…' Panic was beginning to build up inside her. What if he'd just been humouring her? She tried to raise herself up on one elbow but the intravenous line in her arm got in the way.

'Emma's fine, thanks to you.' The dark colour ran up under his tan. 'It was the most criminally stupid thing I've ever seen!' The words rammed home as he viciously enunciated every syllable. 'And the most brave.'

'I didn't think.' She endangered his daughter; he was bound to be angry. His anger couldn't hurt her. She was numb; she didn't feel anything—even when she made herself remember that her body no longer carried their child. Had anyone told him? The odd expression in his eyes as he'd muttered the taut afterthought did puzzle her.

'Tell me something I don't already know.'

The nurse returned with a doctor and Hannah watched as her husband was bustled from the room.

'I didn't expect to see you, Ethan. Aren't you going to fetch Hannah home this morning?'

Ethan nodded as he kissed his mother's cheek. 'I'm on my way.'

'A very roundabout way. What's wrong?' she enquired shrewdly. Her son wasn't a man who showed strain externally, but right now he looked tense enough to snap.

'Hannah was pregnant when the car hit her. She lost the baby,' he said abruptly.

'Oh, my dear, I'm so sorry.'

'She didn't tell you, then,' Ethan muttered. He'd hoped that she'd confided in his mother; he'd wanted to think she'd had a shoulder to cry on. After what had passed between them it didn't surprise him that she hadn't wanted his shoulder.

It was such a lot of grief for one person to bear alone,

and it tore him up to think of her holding onto all that pain. Seeing the sheen of tears in Faith's blue eyes, he turned away and walked to the window. A long way below the city traffic crawled along.

'No. No, she didn't.' Faith watched the tall figure of her son with a thoughtful expression tinged with concern.

'The thing is...' Ethan turned and faced his mother '...every time I try to discuss it she changes the subject. It's as if it never happened,' he said incredulously.

'People have different ways of coping with these things.'

Ethan glared at her with frustrated anger. 'I know that!' he snapped. Taking a deep breath, he controlled his temper. 'She needs help and I don't know how to help her. I don't think she even wants me to help. It's all very well for the doctors to say I have to be patient and not push things.' He snorted impatiently. 'Oh, she talks—she talks to me as if I'm a stranger. She's polite, the way she used to be.' The way he had thought he wanted her to be. 'She's shutting me out.'

'Perhaps it will help being home.'

'I hope so,' he said heavily. 'She misses Emma and Tom,' he admitted. 'Perhaps you're right.'

'Alexa!' Hannah stiffened as she recognised with shock the figure who walked through the door into her anonymous hospital room. 'I was expecting Ethan. I'm going home today.' Home. What had he said? As for this house, you're the hired help.

'What a lot of lovely flowers,' Alexa observed in a brittle tone.

'Yours were lovely, thank you.' She waited tensely to hear what the other woman was doing here. Then thought, why waste time wondering? 'Why did you come, Alexa?' It was pointless pretending—the enmity Alexa felt towards her was out in the open now.

'I did a terrible thing. It was wrong of me, very wrong...' The young woman opposite Alexa sat with a face of stone. There was no encouragement in the calm hazel eyes; there wasn't much of anything. Alexa fumbled in her handbag for a tissue and cleared her throat. She nearly lost her nerve, but the agony of guilt she'd been experiencing made her plough on. 'You saved Emma's life—my grandchild. I lost Catherine. I couldn't bear to lose Emma too. It made me realise how selfish I've been. I've been feeling so guilty.'

And I'm supposed to assuage that guilt by forgiving you, Hannah thought. It would be the mature, adult thing to do, but she wasn't feeling very adult today. The compassion was still there somewhere, but she couldn't tap into the source.

When Hannah didn't respond, Alexa swallowed hard before continuing in a quavering tone, 'When Ethan told me he was taking you away for a belated honeymoon I knew I had to do something. He was Catherine's. It didn't seem right—he belonged to her. Do you see?'

Hannah saw. He still does, she thought. She knew she should feel something—pity, anger, compassion—but she couldn't get past that great empty space inside.

'I could tell something was going on between you, the way he was looking at you, touching you... I lied to him to make him think you were selfish and irresponsible.' The tears flowed unchecked down her cheeks now. 'Can you ever forgive me?'

'It doesn't matter now,' Hannah said in a tight, unemotional voice. Awkwardly she patted the older woman's hand.

The inarticulate sound that escaped Ethan's throat made her look up. 'Ethan!'

Alexa gasped and twisted around. When she saw Ethan standing in the doorway she went deathly pale. 'I didn't mean any harm.'

Ethan's lips were a bloodless gash; his eyes had narrowed to slits. Hannah could see the inner battle he had to control his turbulent emotions before he eventually spoke. 'Get out of my sight.' He closed his eyes as the woman scuttled past him with a sigh of relief.

'What can I say?' he asked Hannah hoarsely.

She shrugged. 'It doesn't matter now.'

'Of course it matters,' Ethan grated. He reached out to touch her arm and she shied away. He couldn't fail to miss the spasm that contorted her features, as if his touch made her skin crawl. He drew a sharp, ragged breath as he momentarily averted his face. 'I had no idea she…' He paused. Words seemed woefully inadequate to express his regret.

'I told you.' The blankness in her eyes was somehow worse than reproach.

'I haven't forgotten. Are you ever going to forgive me?'

'I suppose a resentful wife would make life uncomfortable. Poor Ethan—you didn't bargain for all this when you gave me the job, did you?'

He shook his head from side to side as she spoke. 'Talk to me, Hannah,' he pleaded urgently. 'If you hate me, just come out and say so. Yell at me if you must!'

Hannah just looked at the upturned palms of his outstretched hands and slowly her gaze shifted to his so familiar face. Did she hate him? Was that what happened to love when it went sour?

'I can't perform to order just for you, Ethan. Besides,

what would the nurse say if I started throwing things?' she asked drily as the figure in white appeared behind him.

The wheelchair seemed excessive, but Hannah was quite happy to fall in with hospital policy. Ethan carried the accumulated clutter of her stay, but even as she got into the car he didn't touch her; she noticed that.

'I asked Mother. I thought you might like to see her,' Ethan said as he opened the big front door at home.

'That's nice,' she observed without any real enthusiasm.

The pain started when she walked into the living room. The part inside her which had been frozen started to thaw. The ice had been so tangible, she looked down half expecting to see a pool of water around her feet. The room was full. They all seemed so happy to see her. Faith's new husband was beside her, and Drew. Even Mrs Turner had forgotten her usual reserve. There were flowers everywhere.

'Grandma fetched them for you,' Emma said excitedly when Hannah admired them. 'I baked biscuits for you. Alison helped me.'

Hannah looked incuriously at the tall, strapping figure of the young girl standing in the corner of the room. The girl smiled back shyly. Emma was obviously reluctant to let go of Hannah's hand, but when Ethan motioned her to fetch the plate of home-made biscuits for Hannah she did so.

Hannah was surprised the crumbs would go past the immense, aching constriction in her throat. 'You're all so kind, but it's a bit...'

'Overwhelming,' Faith said, immediately noting the tell-tale signs of disintegration on the drawn face of her daughter-in-law. 'Come on, children, let's go for a walk before tea. Come along, Robert.' She tugged at the arm of the tall, distinguished-looking figure of her new husband. 'Alison, will you get the children's coats on?'

Hannah could hardly see them through the mist of unshed tears that welled hotly in her eyes. Ethan was still there—he was the last person in the world she wanted to display her weakness in front of.

'Who is Alison?' She willed back the tears and even managed a stiff smile.

'A girl from the village. You needed help.'

'You mean Mrs Turner needs help. What's happened to Grace?' Grace was the student who supplemented her grant helping Mrs Turner with some of the domestic chores.

'Not with the house; with the children.'

Hannah's eyes followed him as he walked over to the baby grand piano that sat in the corner of the room. He lifted the lid and played a single chord.

Suddenly her heart was racing with panic and anger. 'Whilst I was in hospital, possibly. I'm home now.' She'd already realised her place here was tenuous. Was he trying to wean the children away from their dependence on her? She loved them as if they were her own and she couldn't even contemplate the idea of losing them. She'd fight Ethan over that.

'You'll still need help.'

'No, I don't,' she insisted belligerently.

Ethan viewed her dogmatic denial with thinly concealed frustration. 'She's well qualified,' he said, as if she hadn't spoken. 'She hopes to get a job in a kindergarten eventually—she was quite honest about that—but as a short-term measure—'

'You're employing her as a nanny?' Hannah asked,

breathing hard. Was this Ethan's brutally efficient way of showing her how dispensable she was?

'She's only doing a few hours a day, but she's quite flexible. I said we didn't want her living in or anything, and I made it quite clear that it was a trial period. If you don't like her—'

'Oh, I still come into it, then!' Breath coming hard and fast, she glared at him with dislike.

'Naturally you still come into it.'

His calm was beginning to infuriate her. 'Why? You've just replaced me the moment my back was turned.'

'That's nonsense and you know it.'

'Don't patronise me, Ethan. Why do we suddenly need a nanny? *I'm* the nanny, in case you've forgotten.'

'You're my wife.'

'I've been your wife for the past year; we didn't need a nanny then. Have you decided I'm not up to the job?'

'I should have done something about it earlier—you need some time for yourself.'

'Oh, I see,' she drawled, 'it's a shift system you have in mind. Are Alison's duties going to take her as far as the bedroom too?'

She had managed to ruffle his tranquillity good and proper this time. The tightening of his mouth had been accompanied by an intimidating flare of fury in his grey eyes. She observed the changes dispassionately.

'I married you. You're my wife,' he snapped, as dark colour seeped up from the collar of his open-necked shirt until his olive-toned skin looked several shades deeper.

'It's not what you did, Ethan,' she said. 'It's *why* you did it. You married me because you wanted someone to care for your children. Someone who expected nothing from you.' Her voice rose until it sounded hysterically shrill in her own ears, but she couldn't stop. It was as if the floodgates had been opened and nothing could prevent the backlog of repressed emotions escaping. 'Everyone must have realised. Faith did,' she babbled wildly. 'That's why she begged you not to marry me. The people you work with talk about us. Did you know that? Do you know how it makes me feel when I think of all those people speculating about us? I feel degraded!'

'I'm sorry if you find being my wife degrading.'

'Being the focus of smutty speculation and pity is degrading!' she yelled back. With the back of her hand she mopped the tears that had begun silently to slide down her cheeks.

'Who pities you?'

'All those smart women that know you, that knew Catherine. They know...'

'Know what?' he asked, taking a step closer.

'What a sham this marriage is. If the baby had lived they'd probably have put it down to immaculate conception.' She stopped abruptly, confusion creeping into her eyes.

Ethan almost sighed with relief. At last. It was the first time she'd actually referred to the lost child. Don't hurry things, he'd told himself. Let her decide when she wants to talk about it. He'd felt impotent listening to the doctor's explanations of denial and the grieving process.

He'd never felt so clumsy and inept in his life. Words were his trade but they came awkwardly now. 'I know it hurts,' he said softly. 'I wish I'd known about the baby.' What was the *right* thing to say? They hadn't told him that, had they?

Anger and resentment moved inside her She'd wanted to tell him. It should have been a time of shared joy but it wouldn't have been like that. She'd been robbed of that too—Ethan's distrust had robbed her.

It was the scent of his cologne which made her realise he was standing close to her. The evocative scent of his male body made her uneasy; it stirred memories she'd carefully blanked out.

'It was very early on. It was only a collection of cells, so tiny,' she said. The pragmatic words didn't help at all; the baby in her mind was whole and perfect. Her lips quivered. 'Why?' she wailed in a small, bereft voice. 'It isn't fair!'

'I know, honey, I know,' he crooned softly as she laid her head against his chest. He could feel the tremors that racked her body as he wrapped his arms around her. 'It's bloody unfair.'

She sobbed out her grief against his chest. When she pulled away Ethan's arms dropped to his sides, letting her go. His heart sank as he saw her expression. It was set and hard. The words she uttered were like a knife-thrust.

'You're probably glad.' In her pain she needed some-one to blame. Part of her registered the intense pain on his face as he flinched. Part of her wanted to reach out for him and deny her words, but the impulse of a wounded animal to strike out was stronger at that mo-ment. 'You don't think I'm responsible enough to look after Emma and Tom. You can take them away from me, but the baby was mine, the only thing in my entire life that's been *mine*. You couldn't have taken him off me.'

'I'd trust you with my life, Hannah.'

She frowned and stared at him in confusion. It was hard not to believe that calm certainty in his voice.

'I trust you with the lives of my children.'

Her resolve hardened as she recalled the awful things he'd accused her of. She couldn't forgive him for being so quick to condemn her. 'You didn't. You believed I put my own pleasure before Emma's safety,' she reminded him stonily. 'You treated me like a leper.' He could have no inkling of how much that had hurt. It had been like being cast out of paradise. At the first hurdle he'd failed the test; he didn't trust her. She'd thought something special had grown between them, but his attitude had shown her what an idiot she'd been to believe that.

'I was a fool!' he said urgently, trying to break past her icy disdain.

'*I'd* be a fool if I believed anything you said to me now. It's easy to be generous when you know the truth, Ethan. Now you know I'm not the selfish slut you accused me of being, what do you want to do? Does this mean a promotion back into your bed?' she suggested with blighting scorn. 'What makes you think I'd want that sort of professional advancement?'

'I know you're hurting, Hannah, but stop this before you say things you'll regret.' His eyes were dark with pain, but she made herself blind to the fact. In the tunnel of her restricted vision all she wanted to see was her own pain and his lack of trust.

'I don't suppose Catherine would have been as crude and…vulgar…' Her eyes went automatically to the walnut bureau where a whole cluster of smiling portraits of her predecessor sat. Her voice died away as she saw, much to her amazement, they had vanished. An antique pewter bowl held a casual arrangement of late, overblown faded roses.

'On the contrary, Hannah, Catherine would have approved of your disgust at the thought of sharing my bed.

We conceived Tom on the only occasion during a six-month period when we slept together. So you see I wasn't exaggerating when I said it had been more than three years. You look shocked.'

'I don't understand.' His words made no sense to her. They'd been the perfect couple—a shining example that she could never aspire to.

'What don't you understand?'

'Everyone says...' The ironic gleam in his eyes made her voice fade uncertainly. 'The pictures... Alexa said...'

'"Alexa said"—oh, then it must be true,' he drawled. 'The pictures were for the children. I didn't want them to forget who their mother was. I owed her that much. Guilt made me go overboard.'

'Guilt?' The bitterness in his voice cut through her miasma of self-pity and aching loss.

'If I'd let our marriage die a natural death, instead of being so bloody-minded and stubborn, Catherine would still be alive.'

Hannah's chaotic thoughts couldn't make sense of the things he was saying. The habit of thinking of his first marriage as perfect was too ingrained to drop immediately.

'I'm not going to force you back into my bed, Hannah. I'm not even going to beg you.'

Of course he wasn't. Ethan didn't have to beg—he was too clever for that. She was awake to the danger she was in. A self-destructive part of her *wanted* to believe in him. Loving Ethan hurt, and she couldn't bear to hurt any more.

'I know you hate me, but don't let your grief twist things.'

'I'm not twisting things; you are.'

'When you're grieving for the baby, Hannah, try and remember that he was my child too. Do you think I don't feel the loss? You don't have a monopoly on grief! I learnt I had a child and I'd lost him in twenty seconds. I nearly lost you.' His voice cracked with emotion. 'I couldn't have borne that, Hannah.'

She took a step away from the message that blazed in his eyes. Why hadn't he said he cared before? she thought angrily. When there was still time. Couldn't he see it was too late now? Everything was spoilt.

'I love you, Hannah.'

'No!' she said, pressing her hands to her ears. 'Don't say that. You bought me, that's all. I'm like any other investment. You can't love me, Ethan. If you did you couldn't have thought all those wicked things about me! You didn't give me a chance.'

'Let me explain,' he begged.

'Nothing you can say could make me feel any different. You set out to make me love you, didn't you?' she accused. His silence spelt out his guilt in her eyes. 'I know you had no use for my love—it was just a way you saw of controlling me. You must have been pleased when your plan worked so well. The irony is you needn't have bothered—you didn't have to lift a finger. I didn't marry you for financial security—I married you because I loved you. I loved you from the first moment I set eyes on you.' She broke off, her bosom heaving with emotion.

The colour drained dramatically from his face as she watched. 'Is that true?' he asked, in a voice she scarcely recognized. He closed his eyes. 'I didn't know. I didn't know…'

Hannah still didn't know what had possessed her to blurt out the truth, but it was too late to deny it now.

'Of course you didn't know—you wouldn't have married me if you had. But don't worry, mistrust and suspicion did what complete neglect couldn't.' Even as she spoke she was suddenly unsure whether her words were actually true. Part of her knew they should be comforting each other through this hard time, not hurting each other.

Ethan turned on his heel and walked towards the window. He missed the quiver of uncertainty that made her lips tremble and filled her eyes with sudden doubt.

'I hear what you're saying.' She saw his broad shoulders lift and then straighten. 'I won't give you any more pain by inflicting my feelings on you, but if you change your mind…I'll be here.'

This was the point where she was meant to say scornfully, I won't. Her mouth opened but she couldn't bring herself to say the words. She stood for a long time staring out of the window after he'd gone. Ethan had said he loved her and she'd sent him away. Hadn't punishing him been meant to make her feel better? She felt wretched, and too confused by the amazing things he'd said to make sense of anything. She started crying and didn't stop for a long time.

CHAPTER NINE

'IT'S Hannah, isn't it?'

Hannah looked blankly at the smart young woman in the fashionable, businesslike trouser suit for a moment. Then recognition dawned.

'*Helen?*' She didn't bother to disguise the incredulity in her voice.

It was hard to reconcile the image of this smart, confident young woman with the girl she had known. Helen hadn't had an easy time after she'd left the children's home.

'You look marvellous, Helen. The last time...'

The young woman grimaced. 'I know. I must have looked pretty desperate, but then turning up on your doorstep out of the blue was an act of desperation. When I saw the announcement of your marriage in the newspaper I didn't have anywhere else to go.'

It was the only time Hannah had gone to Ethan for help. She'd half expected him to be angry, or refuse, but he'd agreed to listen to the girl's story of how she'd been forced out of her bedsit by a landlord who'd been about to sell the building for redevelopment.

All Hannah had been able to think about was that it could so easily have been her standing there with no place to go but the street. 'I hope the place Ethan found you wasn't too awful. I meant to keep in touch, but things have been...' How exactly did you explain the strain of being in love with your husband?

Helen laughed. 'Are you kidding?' she said. 'The trust

has changed my life. They don't just provide a roof and
food; they encourage you to gain skills to go out and
help yourself. Listen, have you got time for a coffee?
I'd love to tell you about it.'

Hannah shrugged. She was escaping; she had nowhere
to go. Originally she'd thought it might be easier to think
away from the house, away from everybody. It hadn't
worked out that way—she'd been wandering around for
the past hour, unable to string two thoughts together.

In the small coffee bar Hannah listened to her friend's
description of the charitable trust that was there to help
young people who would otherwise have ended up on
the streets.

'I'm probably preaching to the converted,' Helen
laughed as she sipped her neglected drink. 'This is stone-
cold. I do go on once I get on my hobby-horse. I'm sure
Ethan has told you all about it.'

'Ethan?' Hannah said blankly. There appeared to be
some sort of conspiracy which prevented her hearing his
name. Not that her memory needed jogging—he was
constantly in her troubled thoughts. She still hadn't come
to terms with his astonishing announcement.

'You're probably cursing me—apparently he's been
giving them a hell of a lot of freebie legal advice at the
moment, with the big legal wrangle. It's a test case, so
it means a lot.' A frown gathered on her face as she
looked at Hannah. 'You don't know what I'm talking
about, do you?' She looked astonished and a little embarrassed. 'I just assumed that you'd know... I didn't
mean to speak out of turn,' she said uncomfortably.

'Ethan's involved with this charity, professionally?'

'He did some research about them when he was looking for somewhere for me to go, and he must have liked
what he found out. He's been giving them free legal

advice since, and that's not something to sneeze at. Have you any idea how much a top barrister like him costs? Are you all right, Hannah?' she asked anxiously.

'I'm stupid.'

'The way I remember it, you were always the bright one at school—the teachers all wanted you to go to college.' The smile died from her lips as she saw the distress on Hannah's face. She planted her elbows squarely on the table and regarded her friend with frowning concern. 'Can I do anything? Do you want to talk about it?'

Hannah's distracted glance was darting and Helen gained the impression that she wasn't actually hearing what she was saying.

'I've been so terrible to him.'

'To who? Ethan?'

'It's probably too late.' Hannah pressed her hand to her quivering lips. What have I done? I love him and I hurt him. I rejected what he was offering. I threw it back in his face. The strong clasp of Helen's hand concentrated her scattered thoughts.

'You could always say you're sorry,' Helen suggested softly.

A tentative smile curved Hannah's lips and a determined light entered her eyes. 'I could, couldn't I?' she said, her mouth setting in a firm line. Sorry wasn't enough, but it was all she had. 'Thank you, thank you so much, Helen.' She pulled a note from her purse and, without even looking at the denomination, flung it on the table. She left the startled young woman staring after her in astonishment.

All she had to do was convince him that she hadn't meant the things she'd said. *All!* Ethan had been an innocent scapegoat for her grief and anger. Since the accident she'd felt as if they'd been slipping further and further apart. The distance that had already develope₍ beforehand had expanded in the emotional, hothous₍ atmosphere of the accident's aftermath until all she coul₍ see was a stranger. Not the man who'd fathered he₍ child, the man she loved.

It was as if seeing Ethan from Helen's perspective ha₍ reminded her of all the things that had been *right* be₍ tween them. She'd spent so long morbidly examinin₍ the negative aspects that she'd forgotten what a warm strong, loving man he was. Ethan wasn't perfect but h₍ came as a package, good points and bad. I'm no bargai₍ myself, she thought wryly.

Did he really say he loved me? she wondered. A sens₍ of wondering disbelief made her almost fall beneath th₍ wheels of a bus. She smilingly brushed away the concer₍ of a passer-by and took several deep breaths. That ha₍ been close! Once might be careless, but twice! She'₍ better be more careful. It would be the ultimate in ba₍ timing to get killed before she'd told him she loved him—especially considering how long she'd been sitting on this particular piece of information.

She'd been walking for ten minutes before it occurred to her that she was on the opposite side of the city to Ethan's chambers. She flagged down a taxi and gave him the address.

'Can I help you?' she was asked on her arrival.

Hannah wasn't in the mood to be intimidated by a superior attitude.

'Yes.'

'Do you have an appointment?' The guardian of the inner sanctum fingered the leather-bound appointment book as if it were sacred.

'No.'

'I'm afraid—'

'I'd like to see my husband.'

'Who exactly is your husband, madam?'

'Ethan Kemp.'

The shift from patronising to deferential was achieved in the space of a single breath. 'I'm afraid Mr Kemp doesn't want to be disturbed today. No exceptions. He refused to see—'

'He'll want to see me.' Hannah picked up the internal phone and held it out. 'Tell him I'm here.' Sometimes pushy worked where nothing else would.

Will he? she wondered. Will he *want* to see me? She maintained her confident stance with great difficulty whilst she strained to catch one side of a low-toned conversation. What will I do if he won't see me?

She wasn't left in suspense for long; the conversation was brief.

'I'll show you the way.'

Hannah wasn't sure why she was feeling relieved—the hard part was yet to come.

Rich oak panelling, one wall covered with books from floor to ceiling, the affluent antiquity of the furnishings sat cheek by jowl with a top-of-the-range computer and fax which was spilling its information unheeded onto the floor as the door closed behind her. The soft sound made her jump.

'I didn't know you were planning a visit.'

'Neither did I,' she confessed.

Ethan was sitting on the edge of the enormous antique desk. He twirled a pen between his fingers and she found the controlled mechanical movement distracting.

'Is there a problem at home?'

'No, not now.' Her reply quelled the brief flare of concern in his eyes. They didn't give anything away now as she screwed up her courage and her nose and thrust her hands deep into the pockets of her jacket.

'You must be wondering why I'm here.'

Her colour was fluctuating from one extreme of the spectrum to the other, and her fingers were spasmodically clenching and unclenching. 'If you don't tell me soon I'd say there's a strong possibility you'll explode,' he observed quietly.

The breath she'd hoarded up escaped her lungs in one audible gasp. 'I came to say sorry and I love you!' She couldn't look at him, but she had to—one eye closed, but the other remaining fixed with anticipation on his face.

Ethan didn't move, but the expensive pen slipped from his fingers. 'You're sorry that you love me?'

'The sorry was for being cruel and mean and despicable to you.' The mingled bronze and green in her eyes misted over emotionally as she opened her eyes earnestly wide in an effort to convince him of her sincerity.

He closed his eyes and let his head fall back. She saw his chest lift as a deep sigh vibrated through his big body. When he lifted his head again some of the tension seemed to have dissolved.

'Family are there so you can be despicable when you're in pain.'

'Am I your family, Ethan?' she whispered huskily, hardly daring to believe what his warm, firm voice was telling her.

'Do you want me to be?'

'I want you to be my heart and soul and...' she began, her voice throbbing passionately. She gave up. Some things words just couldn't express, and, with a sob, she walked into his arms, which opened wide and closed firmly around her. 'I'm so, so sorry...' she murmured as he stroked her hair. 'I've always loved you. I never stopped, even when I was hurting you. I could feel your pain as well as my own, but I couldn't stop all those awful things coming out of my mouth.'

'I've said my share of awful things,' he said, pressing his mouth against the glossy top of her head. 'It's like conkers,' he mused, breathing in the fragrance of the slippery, clean tresses. 'I should have been able to stop your pain and I couldn't. He took her face between his hands and looked into her eyes. 'I did an unkind, selfish thing when I married you, Hannah. It's probably the thing I'm most ashamed of in my life, but, my God, I can't regret it because it's led me here to you.'

His warm lips were strong and tender as they pressed firmly against her own. 'I can't tell you the exact instant I knew I loved you, or the first time I knew how bleak my life would be without you in it. I've lived through an earthquake, but it was nothing compared with the impact of realising I loved you. I've been sitting here...' He gestured towards the leather swivel chair and then shook his head. 'Actually I couldn't sit still. I've been pacing back and forth, trying to compose a winning argument that would convince you to give me a chance. I couldn't do it!' he confessed. 'All I could see was the pain and reproach in your eyes and I knew I was responsible for putting it there.'

Hannah pressed her hands to either side of his head. 'Don't say that!' she said urgently. She couldn't bear to see the dark shadow slip back into his eyes.

She'd been blind to the toll the past days had taken on him up until now, but seeing the dark circles around his eyes, and the deep scoring of the lines between his mouth and nose, made her appreciate that she hadn't been hurting alone. Normally he was the epitome of the sleek, sophisticated professional, but today the designer suit was creased, and a cut which looked suspiciously like a razor cut marred the olive clarity of his cheek.

'It was an accident, Ethan. I shouldn't have blamed you. I know that now. I wanted your baby so badly, but I thought you would be angry after the way you regretted making love to me in the first place.'

With a groan Ethan gathered her close; she could feel the thud of his heartbeat. 'I never regretted making love to you—how could I?' he asked hoarsely. 'I thought *you* regretted it—after all, I did coax, cajole and bully you into my bed. I was mad to believe Alexa and I was blind not to see how jealous her grief over Catherine had made her.' Ethan felt her body stiffen defensively. He stepped back and held her at arm's length.

'It might make you understand better if I tell you a few things about Catherine and myself. No,' he said gently, placing a finger over her lips to stifle her instinctive objections, 'I think you should know. Catherine was beautiful and talented, and at first our marriage was exactly what it appeared. The cracks started appearing when she was pregnant with Emma—she accused me of rushing her into things before she was ready. Her business was flourishing and so was her riding. We got a nanny as soon as Emma was born and things calmed down, but they were never the way they had been. You see, Catherine never really wanted a family, and she resented the fact that I did. Then she discovered she was pregnant with Tom. It wasn't planned and I found out by accident. She'd already booked herself into a clinic,' he recalled, taking a deep, painful breath.

'An abortion?' Hannah tried to compose her features to disguise her shock. Knowing how Ethan felt about his children, she could imagine how devastating that discovery must have been.

Ethan nodded, his eyes desolate as he relived the memory. 'She accused me of engineering the pregnancy deliberately, which, considering she was taking the pill, was an impossibility. I begged her to reconsider, give herself time to think about the consequences of what she was doing. Whatever else it might have been, it wasn't going to be the quick-fix solution she wanted. I knew Catherine, and I honestly didn't think she could have lived with the guilt. She only got as far as the clinic door; she never went inside. Maybe what I said swung it, or maybe she would never have gone through with it anyway.'

'And after Tom was born?'

'She didn't even hold him. She refused to accept professional counselling, and we continued to present the façade of one big happy family!' The bitterness in his voice made Hannah long to comfort him, but she knew he hadn't finished yet, and she instinctively knew he needed to expose what he saw as his shortcomings.

'If Catherine had married someone else she'd probably still be alive now. Someone who hadn't coaxed away her doubts about starting a family. When she kept putting it off I said there was never a perfect time to start.'

It felt strange, feeling pity for someone she'd envied for so long, but Hannah did. 'Lots of women fit families into successful careers, Ethan.'

'Because they *want* to. I convinced myself that deep down she wanted all the things that I did, but she didn't. With Emma, I think it was just a matter of getting it over with as far as she was concerned. Oh, she loved her, but she was never demonstrative. I suppose I resented all the times Emma got pushed into the background. That's why I overreacted when I thought you'd forgotten about Emma—Catherine forgot about Emma all the time.' The bleak way he said it brought tears to Hannah's eyes. 'I tried to compensate, and then Catherine would accuse me of spoiling the child. It was an impossible situation.'

'I think it's likely Catherine was conforming with society's expectations rather than yours when she decided to have a child, Ethan. Women are expected to want children.'

'Are you trying to make me feel better about myself, my love?'

'Am I your love, Ethan?' she asked softly, winding her arms about his neck.

'Do you still want me? I'm a bit of a flawed hero, and you haven't heard the worst yet.'

'You can't get rid of me so easily.' She'd banish the torment from his voice and heart if it took her for ever. She and Ethan had for ever now; the knowledge made her heart soar. 'You'll *never* get rid of me.' Her body vibrated with the deep sincerity of her words. He could save the worst for later—right now the priority was to show him exactly how much she loved him.

'You have no idea how much I've missed holding you, touching you,' he breathed as his lips slid down the side of her neck.

'When I agreed to marry you I never thought you'd love me. I thought I could be satisfied with just being close.'

'And were you?'

'Not once you'd kissed me. Could you kiss me again, Ethan?' she whispered.

'Whilst he willingly obliged, Hannah's fingers were busy flicking open the buttons on his shirt. 'What are you doing?' he gasped throatily when her busy fingers didn't stop there.

Hannah gave a voluptuous sigh and buried her face in the soft hair that was sprinkled over his chest. 'I've not worked out the details yet,' she admitted frankly as she pushed his shirt firmly out of the way, 'but it sort of goes like this...'

Ethan watched through half-closed eyes as she slid to her knees. A harsh, guttural groan was wrenched from the depths of his chest as her mouth touched him.

'Hannah!'

'I thought I'd work out the details as I go along.' It was a liberating feeling, being shameless.

His fingers brushed the top of her glossy head before tangling deep into the soft waves as she became more engrossed in her self-appointed task to drive him insane. 'What are you trying to do to me?'

Her head fell back against his circling hands and she gazed up at him with hot-eyed, sultry provocation. 'I'd have thought that was obvious,' she challenged huskily.

His thumbs were locked at the back of her head. She turned to one side and took one of his fingers inside her mouth, suckling slowly and luxuriously. She felt the muscles in his thighs bunch and tighten as if the relatively innocent action was just as stimulating as the intimacy of seconds before.

'Don't!' she protested weakly as he drew her to her feet. Her legs could hardly bear her weight. Under the light covering of sweat, her body burnt. The burning continued inside too, in the aching hunger that writhed deep in her belly. 'I thought you liked...' Her voice trailed off under the impact of his molten gaze. The pupils had expanded to obliterate almost all of the light grey of his eyes. The driving, almost mindless need she saw there killed off any sudden nagging doubts she'd begun to nourish about offending him. 'Why?'

'I don't want to be the only one who is satisfied.' He'd been tempted by her obvious willingness to set aside her own needs; what man wouldn't have been? 'I want to feel your pleasure too.' He ran a hand that wasn't quite steady down the curve of her cheek. His fingers trailed across her chin before touching the pink outline of her lips. His chest expanded rapidly as her tongue darted out and the sound that emerged from his throat was one of pain.

Hannah could empathise—the pleasure did bring pain, the wrenching pain of anticipation and need. 'It was pleasure,' she assured him throatily. 'You're pleasure, touching you…tasting you. I didn't know just seeing you aroused and knowing I can make you…' She shook her head, still stunned by the discovery that to give pleasure could be just as erotic as receiving it. 'I've fantasised about…' Bands of hot colour flared across her cheek-bones but she didn't remove her luminous eyes from his. 'I didn't know it would feel like—that I would feel like that.' A voluptuous shiver ran through her body and, despite the heat she was generating, goosebumps broke out over the slick surface of her skin.

'Dear God, Hannah!' His mouth devoured the ripe fullness of her soft lips. The raw hunger in him nearly suffocated her with pleasure as his tongue drove with frenzied fervour into the warm moistness of her mouth, and his teeth nipped and bit at the swollen outline of her parted lips. 'Shall I tell you what I've fantasised about?' She wouldn't like it—it might make her hate him—but he had to unburden his guilt.

Hannah's reply was lost in Ethan's hot mouth as he lifted her up and carried her over to the leather chaise longue. The material of her sweater peeled away under the rough eagerness of his hands. Very deliberately he untied the three ribbons that held the thin camisole she wore beneath. There was a taut stillness in him as he looked down at the pale outline of her slender body.

'You're so beautiful,' he breathed thickly.

Hannah was inclined to let this gross misinterpretation of the truth pass—besides, Ethan made her feel beautiful. He made her feel desirable and womanly.

With great care, he parted her thighs. The touch of his hands on her skin made an imprint that went soul-deep. She belonged to this man; she *needed* to belong to him.

'I was going to say it was outside my control, but that's not true.' Like a man being torn in more than one direction, his tortured eyes continued to roam over her body.

'What isn't, darling?' If he didn't touch her soon she'd die. Her desire had pooled into the lower half of her body, making it almost impossible for her brain to function beyond the single imperative message it was screaming. But, despite this, the strangeness in his voice penetrated her passion-fogged mind.

'I knew you could have got pregnant. Like now, I wanted to implant my seed in you, fill you to overflowing.' The words emerged in a strange, disjointed staccato. 'It was selfish, but it overrode every logic circuit in my head. It honestly wasn't like that with Tom—we did take precautions.' He shook his head as if to chase away old, painful memories. 'I don't think you can trust me, Hannah.'

'Why can't I trust you?' she asked gently. It was his deep distress that touched her rather than his words; she was too engrossed by the primal message that sang in her head. 'Make love to me,' she pleaded, reaching out for him.

'Don't you understand what I'm saying?' he asked, staring at her hands. 'Part of me *wanted* you to be pregnant. I *wanted* to see your body grow big with my child. I've never felt like this before in my life, Hannah. I took advantage of your inexperience.'

This catalogue of imagined injuries had gone on long enough. 'Nobody of my age is *that* inexperienced. I knew what could happen, Ethan. You can't really knock a primitive urge which has served the human race pretty well so far. Don't confuse primal with barbarous.'

'I didn't consider how you felt, what you needed!' he continued angrily. 'Even now…I was going to…to ravish you! I can't explain how basic…raw—'

'I didn't know you felt like that too!'

Her husky amazement cut off his soul-searching confessions. 'What did you say?'

'Do you think I have ever imagined doing the things I do with you with anyone else? I'm totally shameless with you and I like it that way. And I'd love to have your baby. The doctors told me there's no reason why we can't…soon.' There was no conflict in the desire that shone out of her eyes. Ethan let out a hoarse cry.

At last! Deprived of his touch for several minutes, she let out a cry of delight as he was upon her. He was within her too, sliding so deeply between her flexed legs that it felt as if they were one.

Ethan retrieved his jacket from the floor and draped it over her shoulders as their sweat-slicked bodies cooled. Hannah gave a sigh of pure contentment as she snuggled against his body. She giggled as he drew the fine grey wool up over her nose.

'Hey, are you trying to suffocate me?' she asked, poking her nose over the top. The teasing smile was replaced by a serious look. He ought to look mellow and relaxed, but she could still see the tension in his lean body. 'I hope the door was locked.'

'Nobody's going to risk disturbing me today.'

'Been a mite tetchy, have you?' she teased lightly.

'I've scandalised the whole building by telling a High Court Judge that I'm too busy to talk to him. I suppose you could call that tetchy.'

'It's more impressive than yelling at the cat.'

'Did you do that?' he asked fondly.

'I would have if we had a cat.' She knew he had something else he wanted to tell her and she was trying to work out how to give him the opening. 'I've been jealous as hell of Catherine ever since I knew she existed.' You could drive a double-decker bus through that particular opening.

'And now?'

'Not jealous.' She felt pity for a confused, unhappy woman. She believed that from Ethan's compulsive need to account for all the crisis points in his tragic marriage would come a lightening of the burden he'd been carrying.

'Catherine always wanted to be the best at everything she did—she was ambitious. I admired it, but it went deeper than simple ambition: she *needed* to be the best. She always enjoyed having her talent publicly recognised; the medals meant a lot to her. Please believe I accepted her wishes, even if I was revolted by the very notion.' His nostrils flared and she could see a pulse throbbing in his temple.

'Of course I believe you.'

'When it came down to it, it was her body not mine.'

He closed his eyes and she saw the muscles in his throat work hard. 'Perhaps I should have kept my mouth shut?'

'You weren't a disinterested party, Ethan.'

'When she accused me of using the baby to cement our relationship perhaps she was right, although I denied it at the time. We'd been drifting apart for some time. She hated being pregnant.'

'Lots of women do, Ethan, but it's worth it in the end.'

'It wasn't the easiest pregnancy,' he admitted, 'and Catherine hated to make concessions to her condition. I tried to coax her to do as the doctors said and that caused quite a lot of conflict. I told you when Tom was born she wouldn't touch him,' he said heavily. 'She wouldn't even look at him. She said I'd wanted him, so I could look after him. The doctor's label was post-natal depression, and it would pass. She didn't live long enough to prove them right or wrong, and I didn't provide the support she needed. But I always knew that the depression was only half the story. There was more to it than that.'

'It must have been terrible—for you both,' Hannah said, tears of compassion glittering in her eyes.

'She said I'd ruined her life—a fairly accurate conclusion given subsequent events.'

'You can't blame yourself for her death, Ethan. It was an accident.'

'She was determined to act as if she'd never been pregnant, not had a baby. That's why she climbed straight back into the saddle; that's why she was racing three weeks after Tom's birth. If I hadn't forbidden her to take that injured rider's mount when Moonlight went lame, she wouldn't have. She knew the brute's reputation; it was too strong for her. She just had to prove to me that I had no control over her life. I can hear her now. "You made me carry him for nine months, Ethan," she said, "but that's the last thing you make me do."'

'She was confused and in pain, Ethan. People hit out when they're in pain. I did.'

'Promise me you'll never shut me out again, Hannah,' he said imperatively.

'Never,' she agreed instantly.

'Have you really been lusting after me since the very beginning?'

Hannah was delighted to see the wide, rather smug grin chase the last remnants of melancholy from his face.

'Lust had nothing to do with it,' she responded firmly.

'Nothing?' he repeated with a pathetic spaniel expression.

'Well, maybe this much,' she relented, holding her thumb and finger a hair's breadth apart. 'The rest was a pure, elevated emotion.'

'That's a bit of a blow.'

'It's easy for you to joke about it, but unrequited love is no laughing matter,' she observed, as someone who'd done it and had the tee shirt.

'It seems to me we wasted a lot of time.' He pulled her thigh over his and stroked the sensitive hollow behind her knee. 'I think we were meant to be together.'

'Why, you closet romantic, you,' she cried with delight. The faint colour that drew attention to the sharp angle of his cheekbones made her smile.

'I was just examining the facts.'

'Of course you were.'

'Top of my list when I interviewed for the post...'

'Was that the one of nanny or wife?' she enquired innocently.

'Less cheek or I'll...'

'You'll what?' she asked huskily, tracing the outline

of her lips with the tip of her tongue. She gave a contented sigh as he swiftly responded to her provocation with a sizzling and very satisfying kiss.

'I'm being deep and profound. Can't you behave for five minutes?'

Hannah turned his wrist and glanced at his watch. 'Right, five minutes it is.'

'I wanted a female past the age of being troubled by romantic entanglements.'

Hannah chuckled. 'I wouldn't repeat this to your mother if I were you.'

'It wasn't my plan,' he acknowledged. 'There were several candidates of a…certain age.'

'You do like treading on thin ice, don't you, my love? I fully intend to be a romantically active granny. So start taking the vitamins now.'

He grinned. 'I passed them over and gave the job to you.'

'Then it must have been fate because it wasn't my startling good looks. I can remember exactly what I was wearing.'

'For some reason the words "grey and shapeless" spring to mind,' he observed slyly.

How unkind! 'Do you mind? That's my best interview suit you're talking about.'

'When I realised you were dating that drippy…'

'I was not dating, and he was very nice!' she exclaimed indignantly.

'I got pretty disturbed at the thought of you walking out. I told myself it was just because the children would miss you, but it was more than that.'

'You're just saying what you think I want to hear!' she accused, lapping up every word.

'Show some respect, woman, I'm baring my soul here.'

'I thought you weren't into all this self-analysis.'

'Do you really think I'm the sort of man who'd marry the nanny just to stop her handing in her notice? I rationalised it every step of the way until I was almost convinced I was acting in everyone's best interests. I didn't want to think there might be anything else behind my desire to keep you around. Something kept telling me that I shouldn't let you go.'

'I'm awful glad you didn't,' she sighed, gazing at him lovingly. It didn't matter to her when he'd fallen in love with her. He loved her now—that was the important thing. 'What are you doing?' she asked as he suddenly leapt up.

He stepped into his trousers as he walked across the room and turned the dial on the wall safe. 'I'm going to have a bonfire,' he said, pulling a document out of the safe. She watched in astonishment as he picked up the heavy lighter from his desk and lit the corner of the thick paper. 'There,' he said with satisfaction as the corner caught alight. He pressed the flaming material into a metal waste-paper basket as the flame took hold.

'Was that...?' She looked to him for confirmation.

'Yes, the pre-nuptial agreement, all three copies. I know the symbolism is a bit clumsy, but...'

Slipping her arms into his jacket, she walked over to him. 'You didn't have to do that, you know.'

'I wanted to. If I trust you with my life, which I do, it follows that I trust you with everything else. It's a bit late to endow you with all my worldly goods, but I do.'

'I'm not interested in your goods, Ethan. It's your heart I have designs on.'

'It's yours, my love,' he said instantly. His arms went

around her and Hannah put her heart and soul into the
tender kiss that went on and on until...

'Is it my imagination or is it raining in here?' she
asked vaguely, as his lips lifted from her own. She held
out her hand and felt the definite touch of water.

'It's real.'

'And what's that noise?' she asked, suddenly conscious of a strident ringing.

'The fire alarm—the one that connects with the fire
station. We had the system put in last year at great ex-
pense.'

'Does that mean the building's on fire? Shouldn't we
be doing something?' She was slowly getting saturated.
She lifted a hand to her wet hair. Calm in the face of a
crisis was impressive, but wasn't Ethan taking it a bit
far?

'The fire, my love, is there.' He nodded in the direction of the smouldering waste-paper basket.

'Oh, my goodness!' she exclaimed, horror-struck.
'You mean you...'

'Triggered the sprinkler and alarm system with my
impromptu bonfire? Yes, I'd say you have the situation
in a nutshell.'

Hannah clasped her hands in agitation. 'We should do
something.' Getting dressed wouldn't be a bad start, she
thought, seeing in her imagination the door being
smashed down at any minute by axe-wielding firemen.
'Don't just stand there—put a shirt on.' She stopped, her
sweater half over her head. 'Are you *laughing*?' He was;
he was actually laughing. 'Well, I'm glad you're happy.
Can you imagine what people will think when they find
out you—?' She broke off. The expression on his face
was jubilant.

'I don't care,' he said simply. 'I don't care what people think, and you know what? It's liberating. You're my liberation, Hannah Kemp, and I'm laughing because I'm happy. I'm happy because you're mine!'

'What are you going to do when the fire service walks through that door?' She tried to sound severe but his frivolity was contagious.

'Tell them to go away. This party is strictly by invitation only.'

'Am I invited?' For some reason she couldn't stop grinning like an idiot.

'To share my life,' he said huskily.

Hannah stopped grinning and began to sob.

'My love, what's wr—?' Gulping back her tears, Hannah pressed her fingertips to his lips. 'Nothing's wrong. You just keep saying such beautiful things,' she wailed. 'And I'm so happy. It's a well-known fact...' she sniffed '...that a person can't cry while being kissed.

Hannah was delighted to discover that her husband, *clever man*, had caught the drift of her subtle hint immediately.

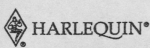

Presenting...

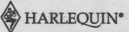

HARLEQUIN®

PRESCRIPTION ROMANCE
Rx

Get swept away by
these warmhearted romances
featuring dedicated doctors
and nurses.

LOVE IS JUST
A HEARTBEAT AWAY!

Available in December
at your favorite retail outlet:

SEVENTH DAUGHTER
by Gill Sanderson
A MILLENNIUM MIRACLE
by Josie Metcalfe
BACHELOR CURE
by Marion Lennox
HER PASSION FOR DR. JONES
by Lillian Darcy

Look for more
Prescription Romances
coming in April 2001.

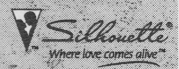

Tyler Brides

It happened one weekend...

Quinn and Molly Spencer are delighted to accept three bookings for their newly opened B&B, Breakfast Inn Bed, located in America's favorite hometown, Tyler, Wisconsin.

But Gina Santori is anything but thrilled to discover her best friend has tricked her into sharing a room with the man who broke her heart eight years ago....

And Delia Mayhew can hardly believe that she's gotten herself locked in the Breakfast Inn Bed basement with the sexiest man in America.

Then there's Rebecca Salter. She's turned up at the Inn in her wedding gown. Minus her groom.

Come home to Tyler for three delightful novellas by three of your favorite authors: Kristine Rolofson, Heather MacAllister and Jacqueline Diamond.